DESTINY WITHOUT DESIRE

DESTINY WITHOUT DESIRE

Defeat of the Curse

Or

The Watermonger-Unwettable Mender

Araman Copa

PARTRIDGE

A Penguin Random House Company

To order additional copies of this book, contact
Partridge India
000 800 10062 62
orders.india@partridgepublishing.com

www.partridgepublishing.com/india

CONTENTS

PROLOGUE

$\mathcal{G}$ood always triumphs over evil in the end; people who follow the path of good generally succeed. This is what has been portrayed in this book. This book encompasses the story of a reluctant young orphan and his friends who, along with an unpredictable, halcyon teacher, embark on an adventure that could be potentially dangerous and life threatening.

Legend has it that the Giants – the only perfect carnivores, are extinct. But who knows whether that's true? Who knows that amidst their own quiet, peaceful existence in the Valley of Fymland, there lived men who kept the very roots and veins of history flowing with pure water and rich blood?

The very existence of other places to the west of Fymland is ignored in the Valley. So when the three friends along with their geography teacher seek to find answers to such questions, they realize the truth of this world. They realize that peace and happiness were not the only virtues of their world. The four elemental Lords come face to face with truth, conceit, deception, bravery, power, war and emotion.

What would their reaction be when they realize the truth about themselves and Mr. Thomas, their geography teacher? Will they accept the challenge which their ancestry had also welcomed? Will Alex, Jack, Jason and Mr. Thomas survive? Will they be able to destroy the Ruby of Ganohan and kill the Giant King Maut? Will good triumph over evil?

The four Lords get trained in their own fields at Iregor, 'The Land of the Lords'. They slowly get introduced to the ethereal concept of magic and the secrets and mysteries of nature. They learn to control their desires, their demands, which could carry them into taking the wrong path; a mistake made by their fathers.

This book also deals with war but in a minor context. War results in nothing but destruction and agony. Albert Dietrich has rightly said, "There are perhaps many causes worth dying for, but to me, certainly, there are none worth killing for." Soldiers fight day and night without any actual material cause. The book speaks about the greater guilt on the part of humanity at not being able to give up wars.

On completing this book, I felt the joy that one feels on accomplishing something. I feel that writing a book is just like an adventure. You get into the book, get out, and become the hero just like the rise and fall of the ocean tide. One can never really write unless he feels it in his gut, unless he feels about his book with pure emotion.

Writing this book has been the joy of my life. It was a great experience and showed me the bounty of language.

ACKNOWLEDGEMENTS

$\mathcal{G}$reat individuals have influenced my life. If not for them, this book would not have blossomed.

I would like to thank my parents, Mr. Upendranath Bhupal and Mrs. Malathi Bhupal for boosting my confidence while writing this book. I would like to thank my sister, Miss Shreeyu Bhupal for giving her valuable inputs. I had got stuck several times, it was she who helped me get out of the labyrinth.

But for my grandparents, I would have completed this book at a much later time. They would ask me about my book and its progress a number of times and I had felt compelled to finish this book as quickly as possible, get it published and then present it before them. I would also like to thank my Uncle and Aunt who advised me various times on how the knowledge required to write a book should be gained.

Once again the great confidence provided by my school friends kept me going on this literary adventure. I would like to express my sincere gratitude to my class-teacher who is also my English language teacher, Mrs. Antara Dutta of North Point School, Navi Mumbai. It was she who taught me the semantics of the language.

I would also like to thank my football coach Mr. Purushottam who knew in advance of the slow birth of this book and motivated me.

From the bottom of my heart, I thank my mother. It was she who saw this talent in me. With her constant support and reassurance, I was able to carry myself like a budding author.

Once more I would like to thank my father who took charge of the editing of this book and furnished me with his expertise. He helped me in the polishing of my manuscript. If not for him, this book would never have taken its current form.

I would also like to express my sincere gratitude to the people at Partridge Publishing Penguin Books India Private Limited for eventually reaching this book to the readers.

I quote W.T. Purkiser in the above context– "Not what we say about our blessings, but how we use them is the true measure of our thanksgiving."

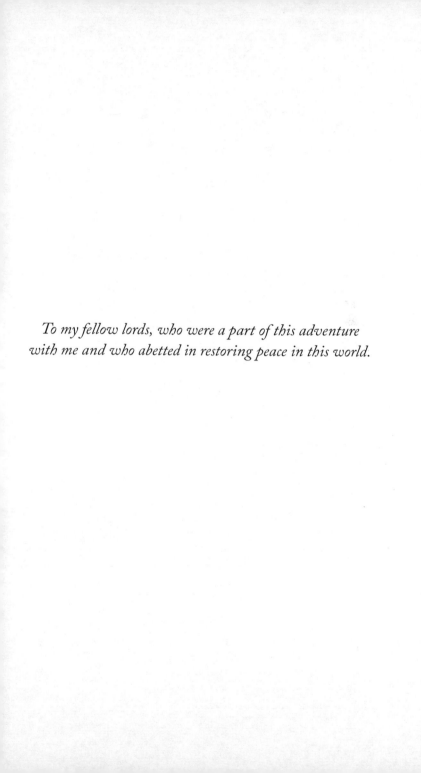

To my fellow lords, who were a part of this adventure with me and who abetted in restoring peace in this world.

CHAPTER 1

School trip to Sumter Fort

I never wanted to embark on an adventure. But destiny had it in store for me.

It is said that if one believes in the legends of one's land, one ends up following the path taken by one's ancestors. The brave and the mighty are always exemplified by a few whose passions are aroused by mythology. Sometimes it is the passion and at times it is the destiny.

Being an adventurer is not at all easy; it's brutally tough and scary. It's the grit and nerves of steel that keeps an adventurer going and eventually succeed in his mission.

My name is Alexander. I am called Alex by the ones close to me. I don't have a last name.

I am sixteen years old. I am an orphan taken in by the Flareds Academy, a private orphanage for nameless kids in upstate Rollingham, Lower Fymland Valley.

Am I an orphan and a nameless kid? Only time will tell.

Yes, you could say that for the moment. This very thought pricks my mind all the time and makes me testy in my disposition to others. I am a bit eccentric when it comes to studies – sometimes unusually good and at times abysmally bad.

All my teachers, except one, take me for a rebel because of my crabby nature. And the exception is my geography teacher, Mr. Thomas. He likes my idiosyncrasies – brushing my hair with my left hand and looking people in the eye without hesitation. I feel a connection with him whenever we make eye contact.

The only people close to me at Flareds are my friends Jack and Jason and my geography teacher, Mr. Thomas.

Mr. Thomas is a middle aged guy with unkempt hair and a muscular body who always wore a black leather jacket which smelled of cupcakes. He always cracked jokes and lightened the moods of students during tough times. He was an ailurophile. My best friends and also my roommates, Jack and Jason who are orphans like me, are of cheerful nature. All our teachers liked them because of their amenable temperament.

It was the third Saturday of May. I got up early along with Jack and Jason to pack our bags. We had a one-day school trip to Sumter fort. We had never seen or heard anything about Sumter Fort and as such we were enthusiastic.

The whole eleventh grade was interested for the trip except a few (read 'book worms') who kept muttering that the trip was going to be boring. We were going to be accompanied by two teachers. Unfortunately one was Mrs. Philips, our least favorite teacher who taught us Science and Math. Fortunately Mr. Thomas was accompanying us too, so we had hopes.

We were quickly done with the morning ablutions and wore our dresses while whistling together a song on 'joy of life'. I wore a blue colored T-shirt and half pants. This was the only good outfit I had. We hastily checked our back packs. I had kept two bottles filled with water, a cap, an extra T-shirt, a magnifying glass, a torch, a notebook, a pencil and a map of the sort. I always kept a magnifying glass with me as I always felt that it might be needed. But till now it was of no use on any of our trips arranged by the orphanage (hardly any).

We locked our room and then hurried to the stilt area where the whole batch was assembling. In our course, we found Mr. Thomas with his hands inside his pockets. He wore a green colored shirt inside his usual black colored jacket over black trousers and a Sun-hat over his head which hid his eyes. In short, he looked like a zombie.

"Good Morning Mr. Thomas." I said as he approached us.

"Oh, yes, without a doubt it is a good morning." He said, "The trip should be fascinating."

"It should be Mr. Thomas, we are all excited." said Jason.

"Okay then, I`ll meet you in the stilt area," saying that Mr. Thomas advanced towards his room.

***

"At last we set off!" said Jason. We were sitting in a rickety Bus that was true to its name - 'The B Star'. It had been hired by our orphanage for a bargain. Having dents on its flanks, tattered seats and cracked floor it looked like a bus which had been restored recently after an accident. Most of the time I wondered what will happen if the floor suddenly gave way.

We had set off from our orphanage half an hour ago and were now passing through the country side. We had travelled twenty miles since we left our orphanage and were told by the driver that Sumter Fort was another hour away. I wondered if we the bus would last the journey. But it did!

Jason and Jack kept talking about the fort – its massive size, bastions and the moss on its rocky structure. They were even more cheerful today and were talking in excited voices.

***

First thing on priority for all of us upon reaching the Fort was to open the breakfast packets and devour the contents, which we did ravenously sitting on the lawns.

It was indeed a big fort – a massive five storied structure made of brown colored stones between which weeds grew. Columns of creepers ran along the walls of the fort. It had seven gates out of which five were still in good shape. There was a path that led to the inside of the fort. At the entrance to the fort there was a massive solid arch with balconies on the flanks accessed by series of steps on either side.

"It's impressive." I said.

The fort walls formed the western boundaries of the lower valley beyond which no one was permitted to go for a reason that was not forthcoming. The Egilium forest mainly formed the fort's surroundings amidst which a lake was fed by the rushing waters of the river Egil.

"All of you listen to me," called Mrs. Philips, "this fort was built two hundred years ago by Dane, the king of Fymland. You can see that despite its age the structure is still rugged and tough."

All the children nodded their heads. They were eager for more information. Everyone's face shone with excitement. Even the 'book worms' who were not interested in the visit were excited and impressed by the visual impact of the structure. Mrs. Philips however, had a pale face as always but now for a change she wore a little smile. As for Mr. Thomas, his face shone with happiness as if he had taken a breath of fresh air for the first time after coming out of a coffin.

The fort was located on the top of the "Riveria Hill", west of the lower valley. I looked down to the valley of Fymland which from the top looked like a vast brown ocean. I exclaimed at this beautiful view. As if reading my thoughts Mr. Thomas said, "It is a beautiful view, isn't it? But the Fymland valley is not as big as it seems to be. You haven't seen the world my boy." His words aroused in me a fleeting wish to see the world beyond Fymland.

"This is going to be fun," said he as he entered the fort followed by Mrs. Philips and seventy-two children.

CHAPTER 2

Battle of the Sumter Fort

After passing the massive arch, I realized that the fort was not as big as it seemed. I remembered that what appears to the naked eye could be an illusion as looks can be deceptive.

It consisted only of the fort walls which encircled the central courtyard having guard rooms, which were also combined with many bastions and mounted by cannons, and the citadel. The cannons were also lined along the approach path to the citadel. When I looked at the fort walls closely, I found cracks in which weeds grew. Apart from the weeds I saw some grain sized particles sticking to the wall surfaces. These were golden colored specks which felt metallic to the touch. I wondered what these were. However, these remained a mystery only for a while.

All the time I was in the fort I felt that however small it was, it was in some way very well planned. The arches, the cannons, and the bastions everything seemed to fascinate me. I felt the Fort suddenly unraveled.

Apart from us there were many tourists; most of them I suppose must have come from the upper valley of Fymland. The people of the upper valley were brown, dark haired and huge. In contrast, the people of the lower valley were fair and less muscular.

A lady, who I passed, smiled at me courteously. She seemed to be from the upper valley. She was beautiful, but stony pale. Once back in Rollingham, I had attended a wake of a dead classmate. I remembered the lifeless body of the young girl in the open casket.

Her face had been made up charmingly which I had found terrifying. This woman reminded me of that girl except that her eyes were open. I smiled back at her and moved on quietly.

Mr. Thomas seemed to enjoy the trip very much. His face gleamed like summer. However, within that happy face I could see something which no other person could see - sadness; sadness which was shown only when the most important thing in the world was lost.

I couldn't even imagine Mr. Thomas being sad. He was a jovial kind of a person. He could even make depressed students buoyant. So, **"Mr. Thomas being sad"** is a phrase in our orphanage which is compared to saying **"Alex is an amenable person."** It doesn't sound real.

We reached the citadel. Its corridors were lined with many statues of Dane and his ancestors. One of them depicted Dane's killing of a Giant double his size.

Others depicted Dane sitting on a horse, making a benign gesture and the like. All these sculptures carried epithets that described King Dane's victories in the various battles fought by him.

Most of the atmosphere in the fort was filled with Mrs. Philips's hoarse voice. She was explaining to us the "Last Battle of Dane" which is also called the "Battle of the Sumter Fort". She was saying- "You all know who Dane was. He was the greatest ruler of our motherland -- the valley of Fymland. This fort here was built during his reign. Fymland owes Dane a large credit for building this fort. This fort has protected the country from the wrath of giants who are extinct today. According to the legend Dane had passed these very boundaries and had crossed the Egilium forests to Ganohan -- the land of Giants ruled by King Maut. He had risked his life doing so because Giants showed immense hatred toward us. He stole from them the great treasure of Ganohan and their most precious thing - the ruby of Ganohan, after distracting the Giant King Maut by killing his son. He had narrowly escaped from Ganohan. This adventure had later cost his life."

"Fymland grew very rich after this battle. This was the time when Fymland was also called 'The Land of Immeasurable Wealth'".

She was interrupted by the undertones of the students discussing amongst themselves. She glared at them resulting in their immediate silence. She then continued - "Within a year's time there was a massive attack by the Giants on the western borders. The reason was the death of the Giant King's son. The army of Fymland had been defeated very quickly and easily. But Dane had defended Fymland standing here on this very land by killing many Giants. He ran as swift as the wind; his blows as powerful as the blows of two Giants. He defended our land till his last breath. His cairn was built on this boundary. While breathing his last he made a new rule for us that no one should cross the western borders of Fymland except his own line. There are no children of Dane that we know. So, we have no trade relations with the valleys beyond the western borders (if any) but trade flourishes with the valleys beyond the northern, eastern and the southern borders. After his death a council was formed that created our constitution and took upon all the legal matters."

A young halcyon boy named Nate asked, "Mrs. Philips, how do you know for sure that King Dane has no progeny?"

Mrs. Philips said, "It's not me Nate. That's what the history books tell us. Don't you read your books properly?" Mrs. Philips snapped.

"Yes Ma'am," replied all at once.

Then I asked her, "Are there really no Giants today Mrs. Philips?"

"There are no Giants as said in the history books. Does that make you happy? Okay boys, it's time for departure now."

CHAPTER 3

The Council of Four

$\mathcal{L}$eaving the fort made me a bit sad. My orphanage was my home; true, but I hated living there. For the first time in my life I felt a connection with this Fort. I felt as if I had a certain propinquity towards it. I couldn't tell why. This short trip to the Fort somehow made me yearn to explore more of it. There was a hint in the air that told me that there is going to be a revelation for us here. Or you could say it was intuition that made me feel this way about the Fort. Naturally, I wanted to explore the Fort with my friends and Mr. Thomas.

Mrs. Philips' narration made me curious. If it is not folklore then, the extinction of all the Giants felt absurd to me. However powerful Dane had been it would not have been possible for him to kill all the Giants. Some Giants, I believed still existed.

"Don't you think Mr. Thomas?" I asked as we headed toward the exit of the Fort.

"I think what?" asked Mr. Thomas.

"That the giants still exist."

"Actually yes, I think they could be still alive today. It is ridiculous to propose that a human, though he may be King Dane, vanquished and slaughtered mighty creatures like the Giants. But the King was not alone you see, he had the whole army of Fymland with him." I caught a hint of a lie as he spoke.

"But Mrs. Philips said that the army had been defeated very quickly and easily by the Giants. So there was no chance for Dane to kill all the giants." Jason said.

"That makes sense." I said.

"The giants should still exist," said Jack.

"Well I don't know about that but as the story goes, King Dane made them all perish." Mr. Thomas said and waved his hand as if not interested in the conversation any more.

"Well, I neither believe in that story nor in the legend of immeasurable wealth." I said arrogantly.

"Then, why do you believe in the Giants."

"I don't believe in the Giants. I meant to say that if Dane or the Giants really existed sometime in the past and the battle of Sumter Fort had happened then, some Giants could exist even today." A whole army of the beasts could not have been wiped out; that's impossible.

"You may be right, who knows. But the story is true." Our conversation was interrupted by Mrs. Philips asking us to hurry up.

It was true, I never believed in the legend. It just didn't seem to convince me. I felt that there was never in existence a ruby of Ganohan. But the name of the ruby made me aware of my inner-self, the soul. Why does the soul get stirred just by the pronouncement of the phrase – "Ruby of Ganohan."

I felt the urge to find answers. Where were the great treasure and the ruby of Ganohan now? Mrs. Philips had mentioned nothing about their whereabouts after the war. If the Giants were dead then the council must have access to these treasures. But she had not mentioned the council acquiring these after the war. This could only mean that the treasures are certainly in the possession of Giants and that they still exist. Looking at it any other way could mean that everything about the story and the legend is false; there never was any Dane or any Giants. The whole legend seemed to be untoward. *Then what was the truth?*

"Mr. Thomas, where is the Ruby of Ganohan if the Giants are extinct?" I blurted.

Jack and Jason who were walking along with us suddenly became interested. Jason and Jack asked in unison, "Oh yes, where is it?" I could see that the mystery was working quite well on them too.

"With the council", Mr. Thomas said, as if it was obvious.

"As far as I remember Mrs. Philips had not mentioned anything about the council appropriating it." I said.

"Well I know nothing about history, so you should better ask Mrs. Philips about it. But undoubtedly this question interests me", said Mr. Thomas rubbing his thick beard.

"And undoubtedly the answer must be the Giants." I said.

"How can Giants be the answer?" he paused and then continued, "wait, are you seriously thinking that the ruby is with the Giants in the present day context."

"Yes!"

"But that's not possible!"

"Why not? It's pretty logical."

"But the Giants do not exist today."

"How can you say that?"

"I am saying what the historians have said."

"Oh, Mr. Thomas please get out of your ethical history. What if the story has gaps?"

"Well, well, I know where you're getting."

"I am not getting anywhere. I just want to prove to you that everything about the story and the legend of immeasurable wealth is false. There were no Giants and there was no Dane. Everything the town folks say is just folklore."

"It is true. And when I say it is true, it is!" He stressed the last words and glared at me viciously.

"Enough you two. Chill now." Jack said trying to calm us both; he couldn't succeed.

"It is utter foolishness." I said showing a contortion on my face which Mr. Thomas more or less did not like.

"It is not." He glared at me again and this time more viciously. Something was wrong. Mr. Thomas was never so ignorant. What was the thing that was blinding Mr. Thomas from the obvious truth? Or is he deliberately looking the other way? I could see a hint of sadness in his eyes. Suddenly, realizing the truth, I asked him, "Mr. Thomas do you like this fort?"

"Yes I like it, in fact very much." He answered.

"You don't want to leave the fort, do you?"

"You're right; I don't want to leave the fort. But I'll have to."

"Is this the reason why you're sad?"

"No, this is not the reason." Okay, I concede. "You could be right but there is no way any of us could prove it."

"Then what can we do to find answers?"

"There might be a way. But you'll know what to do when the time comes."

"Oh, please come back to the present times," said Jason enthusiastically. What should we do now?

Suddenly, something else flickered in my mind, a question which was more effective on Mr. Thomas this time.

"What about the western borders." I asked him.

He swerved toward me and said, "We are banned from crossing it."

"Why?"

"Because of the orders of King Dane."

"I know that but why did Dane decree that?"

"How would I know?"

"If all the Giants were dead why would he ban us from crossing the western borders?"

"Um-uhm, you have a point there mate."

"It makes sense. If all the Giants are dead then why should we not cross the borders? This again tells the same thing – that the story is mythical." This time he did not get angry. He found some sense in my words.

In reply he said, "Okay let's consider for a while that whatever you are saying is right, but how will you convince the whole of Fymland? They think that the story is as true as the truth of their existence. We need hard physical evidence."

There was an air of silence. Everyone was lost in thought. What Mr. Thomas said was right. It was very difficult to convince the people of Fymland otherwise. All of a sudden the silence was broken by the intelligence of Jack: "We should search this fort for clues."

"Let's do it then," said Jason enthusiastically.

CHAPTER 4

The Search

"**B**ut not the whole Fort, we should only search the citadel as it is the closest to the western boundaries," Mr. Thomas said. I hadn't thought of it before, Jack and Mr. Thomas were right. If that great battle was fought on the grounds of Sumter Fort, then there had to be some hidden evidence of its occurrence. That was all we needed. But a question troubled me. I asked everyone, "How do we get time to dig out facts?"

"Yeah, the same question troubles me. We are returning to the Flareds now. Once we get back we will never return to this place. All your enthusiasm was in vain Jack," said Jason.

"Oh! Don't worry about that." Mr. Thomas said good-humoredly, "I'll take care of it. I have a plan. So here it is…"

The plan was something that astonished me, Jack and Jason. It was so good that we could search the Fort as well as take Mrs. Philips' permission for doing so. A single arrow for two birds! But at the same time it was amusing because the sly idea came from a teacher. However, the plan worked out quite well. It went like this:

"Mrs. Philips, Could I go back inside the fort?" I asked her as we exited the fort.

"Why Mr. Alex? If I may ask."

"I have forgotten my magnifying glass."

"Oh, but you can't go there alone."

"Don't worry, I'll go with him," said Mr. Thomas.

"And we too," said Jack and Jason in unison.

"You two don't need to go," said Mrs. Philips to Jack and Jason. Jack and Jason instantly wore a sad look. To their delight Mr. Thomas said, "Oh! Come on Mrs. Philips. You can't be so strict. Let them come along. I'll take care of them too."

"Okay then, go back and come fast. You haven't got much time. Now off you go!"

Mr. Thomas had lied. Teachers taught us that lying is bad and here we have a teacher lying. Could he do that without an underlying noble intention? We will find out soon.

We hurried to the citadel which was apparently the place closest to the western borders. It was naturally ensured by the structure of the fort that Mrs. Philips and others could not see what we were actually doing.

Searching the citadel was not as easy as we thought. Together we sweated a gallon. We searched the citadel from speckle to spot. While searching the walls I again found that golden metallic powder. I tried to pass my hand through the crack and grab some of the powder but in vain. I tried once again and this time I succeeded. I seized the powder tightly and got my hand out.

I examined closely and found it to be genuinely comprised of gold filings. This was puzzling. Why would gold be present on the walls of a Fort? I called for everyone and showed them what I had found.

"This baffles me," said Mr. Thomas.

"Yeah, me too," I said.

"Gold? But how?" asked Jason.

"That's what we have to find out," Jack said earnestly.

"Well we'll find it out afterwards. It's not important right now." I said and asked, "What did you find in your search Jack?"

"I found nothing." Jack said sadly.

"You Jason?"

"The same as you, gold filings." Jason said.

"And you Mr. Thomas?"

"The same as Jack. Nothing," said Mr. Thomas with an expressionless face.

"Well then we are left with the gold filings as our only clue." I said.

"But unfortunately that does not give us any hint," said Mr. Thomas.

"Wait! The gold filings remind me of something. Are we missing anything?"

"I don't think so," said Jason.

"Yes we are!" Jack paused and then continued, "The statues of Dane and his ancestors. Did we search them?"

"No we didn't," answered Mr. Thomas.

"Oh, Yes!" Jason exclaimed.

"Let's try moving them one by one," Jack said. We hurried to the statues and acted on Jack's idea. Most of the statues did not budge. But then Jason found out that the last one did.

"Everyone come here," Jason called. "This statue moved a little." The statue showed the killing of a Giant by Dane. We tried to move it but it did move only slightly.

"Even this does not move. We have lost all the chances," saying that Jason rested on the hilt of the sword of Dane. Suddenly, it went down straight through the chest of the giant lying under, as if showing us a live act of the killing which made Jason stumble. Then came a rumbling sound. The rumbling sound was of the movement of the statue. The statue moved sideways revealing a hole which had a flight of stairs that led down.

Every one of us was bewildered. Jack's mouth was hung open in stupefaction. There was complete silence. Jason broke the silence by saying, "Okay, maybe I am wrong."

CHAPTER 5

Underground

"Yes, you are wrong," I said

"What's down there?" Asked Jack who was a bit unsettled by the motion of the statue?

"How would we know that? Silly of you." Said Jason nonchalantly.

"The only way to find out is by going down." Mr. Thomas said. He paused, looked up at everyone and then continued, "Let's go down. Are you all ready?"

Jack and Jason nodded. But I didn't, instead I said, "Wait, remind me once again, why are we doing this?"

"To find answers." Jason said who was surprised by my question.

"What answers?"

"Answers that could reveal the truth about the story of the last battle of Dane," said Jack.

"Oh is it?"

Then Mr. Thomas asked seriously, "Alex, are you trying to step back?" There came no answer from me so he continued, "I always thought that you were a boy as fearless as Dane."

"Mr. Thomas you are mistaken", I said immediately, "I am not scared I just want to tell that whatever we are doing would not gain us anything. I think we should head back to the bus now."

"When did you start talking about gaining, Alex?" Even Jason spoke now.

"This very minute," I answered back.

The next person to speak was Jack, "This could only mean that you are scared to enter the hole."

"Thanks for the inference," I said sarcastically. This was unusually me.

"Forget about gaining. You are talking about returning to the Flareds! Do you want to spend your entire life listening to tirades from Mrs. Philips?" said Mr. Thomas who by now was glaring at me. I was a bit confused. Why was Mr. Thomas, a well-respected teacher in the Flareds academy, speaking like this? Then again I did not respond to his question so he continued: "Let's try to make it simpler. This might be an adventure Alex! So be convinced."

"Now, come on Alex," both Jason and Jack said. Since the majority voted to proceed, I said "Okay, let's go."

Jack wanted to go first, so he did. After Jack went Jason. "I'll go after you, Mr. Thomas," I said. Returning to the Flareds was now becoming more and more tempting for me as I was not convinced that this passage would lead us anywhere.

"Okay, as you wish," he said. Just then I heard footsteps coming right to the citadel.

"Hurry up Mr. Thomas, someone's coming," saying that I hastily pushed him right into the hole. I glanced around for the last time and hoping that the statue would automatically return to its position I too went down the hole.

I was climbing down the stairs which seemed to be stretching infinitely. I looked up and could see nothing. I sighed. I was lucky. There was nowhere a glint of light to be seen. I looked down, again to see nothing. The darkness made Mr. Thomas say: "will we ever reach the bottom?" "Yeah, someday we sure will," said I to him laughing in the darkness. Not returning to the Flareds and missing Mrs. Philips for the time being had made me less testy and put a smile on my face.

With mixed feelings I too reached the bottom at last. Reaching the bottom gave us all a big relief as we were in no condition to move further. I sat down, grunting. "Hey guys," I called out into the darkness.

"Hello Alex, welcome underground," Mr. Thomas called out.

"Can you help me to my feet, Alex?" Mr. Thomas said.

"Yes, I could help you...but where are you?"

"Oh, this darkness.......Then let me be," Mr. Thomas said. I stood up.

"Where are Jack and Jason?" I asked.

"Right beside you." Both Jack and Jason said in unison.

"So where do we head from here?"

"Let's try heading up straight and stay close to each other," said Mr. Thomas.

We walked and walked never to stop. The tunnel seemed to be an endless conduit of darkness. Somewhere from above, a drop of water fell on my face. So I guessed the ceiling was leaking somewhere far above. Many a time some of us fell hard upon a rock and sometimes hit the wall beside us. This gave us an idea that the tunnel was very narrow. I heard exclamations twice -"Ouch" and "Oh" from Jack and Jason. This underground ramble was becoming a drag and sapping our energy. We were thirsty and exhausted.

Suddenly, there was a fluttering noise in the tunnel. Everyone shouted – "What the hell is that?" We all ducked waiting in expectation. The noise came back from the opposite direction and vanished. We felt a mass of something zooming past us.

"Could be bats guys," said Mr. Thomas, "nothing to worry about."

"Bats could be our ticket to the exit, Mr. Thomas," said I.

"I agree. Then we are moving in the right direction. Let's proceed." said Mr. Thomas.

After about an hour we saw a glint of light in the distance at an angle. Our spirits rose when we had actually begun to doubt the 'bats theory'. Indeed the flying mass must have been of bats.

We hurried toward the direction. As we were reaching the location we found that the tunnel was branching at the light source. The light was emanating from the branch tunnel and the tunnel straight ahead was again pitch dark. The light was orange in color and bore a texture that was possible only if it was reflected from an object – a metal. What metal could that be?

This also meant that we were nowhere near the exit but heading into another tunnel. And were the bats living in this branch tunnel?

We took a turn toward the light source into the branch tunnel. What we saw was truly mindboggling... We had entered a cavern full of gold.

CHAPTER 6

A Cavern of Gold

I say it once again, what we saw was truly mindboggling. The underground tunnel had opened into a cavern full of gold. This must be the Great Treasure! And we had at last found it! Torches were burning inside the cavern. A thick oil was seen to be continuously fed from somewhere above through channels carved out in cavern walls. The gold radiated such bright light that we had to close our eyes at first. Any human (or Giant for that matter) who happens to see this would be desperate to get all the gold in the cavern. But somehow the pangs of greed did not overwhelm us.

Our shadows danced on the walls of the cavern like ghosts. It was something what you might call a house of gold. It was dome shaped, surrounded by walls having a golden hue all over. At a little distance from where I was standing rose a platform. The platform was carpeted with gold coins and the collection included crowns, swords and armor, all made of gold. Why would armor be made of gold except for hanging on walls for display of wealth? We had no answer to that question.

Just then I remembered the ruby of Ganohan. It was nowhere to be seen. I looked for it everywhere, but still could not find it. Finally I asked, "So where is the ruby?"

"It might be somewhere in this cavern," Jack said.

"But it's not here," I said immediately.

"If this is the Great treasure, then the ruby must be here."

Then Jason interrupted picking up one of the gold coins, "no, the ruby will not be here."

"How can you say that?" asked Jack.

"Because this is not the Great treasure. Look at these coins. They show the symbol of Fymland, which means-", he paused. Then Mr. Thomas continued for him, "Which means this is the national treasury of Fymland."

"Why is it not with the council then?" Jack asked.

"Maybe they don't know about its existence," Roalf answered.

"Then we should tell them," I interrupted him.

Whether or not one believes in intuition, I certainly did. As if being drawn towards it, I turned...

To my astonishment, I saw a seven foot monster standing there in the far corner of the cavern. He glared at us. His eyes were red with blood. A stream of thick saliva poured down from its mouth making the floor filthy. His outfit was quite catchy. He just wore loose pants with his upper body bare. His potbelly stomach poured out. I gasped, "What's…that?"

No one answered. The silence was too peculiar. An air of obscurity prevailed.

"A…monster" Jack managed.

At length the creature spoke. "I've been too hungry for a while. It seems like aeons. Your stubborn king tricked me into this cavern and I've been starving since then."

The creature spoke with such hatred and malice that it took the soul out of me. Its voice, an absurd mix of cough and growls, stirred the blood flowing through my veins. I literally felt goosebumps. A foul smell filled the cavern.

Gathering some grit, Mr. Thomas demanded, "Who are you and what are you doing here?"

"Oh! It's you then. I caught the smell. It's the same as before, my dear old enemy." The beast spoke laughing.

"What are you speaking beast? I haven't met you before. But it seems that you belong to that immoral, cursed race." Mr. Thomas spoke with such hatred that I didn't believe my ears. But how was he an enemy to the monster. Immoral race…What did that mean?

"Save your words. You'll need them in hell. I'll devour you first and then the others." It said.

I kept quiet. Fear had launched me into speechlessness. Jason pleaded, "Please, let us go. We'll not trouble you anymore. Please," his voice trailed off as the creature laughed.

"Don't worry. It will be quick and less painful. Your death will be ephemeral. Come, I'll eat you."

"Well that seems to be taking us for granted." Jack said. Man, he had some guts. The creature launched ahead. We ran helter-skelter in all different directions in the room. But Mr. Thomas stood there, keeping his ground. I awed at him.

He wrestled with the monster. But there was something wrong with the way he fought. It seemed as if he was deliberately trying to avoid attention. He was obviously not a trained wrestler. But still…

He was thrown backwards by the beast. It was too much for me to see. I closed my eyes. He yelled in pain. Instantly I was off to help him.

The beast ran towards him. Somewhere from beside, Mr. Thomas had found a sword. He was still lying on the ground. The beast jumped above him. Mr. Thomas raised his sword.

There was one clear sharp piercing sound and then there was silence. Everything was as still as the dark of night. I stopped dead. The beast crumpled to dust.

I had developed a new found respect for Mr. Thomas. He had saved the day.

I walked towards him and helped him to his feet. I kicked the dust in hatred but it filled me with guilt. Mr. Thomas had killed a creature. But that didn't matter because he had done that for his defense. He was a cynosure for me.

Jason had a big smile on his face. He hugged Mr. Thomas tightly and whispered a "Thank You." Jack looked as if he was scared out of his life. We joined Jason and Mr. Thomas.

I replayed, in my mind, all the events that had occurred till now. For the last two hours, I had been through excitement, wonder and what seemed like remorse. Yes remorse. Part of me was prompting me to turn back and return straight to the ground above. But there was something in me which urged me to move on.

It was hope, I guessed. A hope, to find a better life. That was what was urging me to move on. I was tired of this life. As a kid I had extreme feelings. I hated the Flareds for its facilities and boring life. I was always restless there. Anything interesting hardly happened. Now, being away from the orphanage, I had calmed down a bit.

The corner of my eye caught something. My friends followed my gaze. I walked towards the nearby wall. Specks of red paint were visible on it. But something else had drawn my attention. On the wall was written something in red paint too. I was pretty sure it wasn't there before. It read:

"The land of the lords shall lead you to victory." What did it mean? It left me scratching my head. The land of the lords…Who were they? And what did victory symbolize? Sure we were not going to fight any battle or something like that. "You have to find those answers." My soul told me.

First things first. Where had that come from and who had written that on the wall? This was the major question that troubled me.

Jack broke into my thoughts, "Why would Dane hide it from the council? He surely did not mention anything about this on his deathbed. If he had, then this would not have been here. So where is the great treasure?"

"I don't think that the council is unaware of this," said Mr. Thomas, "May be the council has used this cavern as a locker to keep Fymland's national treasury."

"This makes sense", I said to myself, "Mr. Thomas may be right."

Just then as if reading my thoughts a voice said, "And 'Thomas' is right." A form shimmered into existence in front of me out of nowhere. It was someone I didn't know. His tall body was a thin framework of bones. He had keen eyes and a pointed nose. His hair, a hue of grey and white, fell freely on his shoulders. His white beard extended up to his chest. His lanky frame was draped with a long white gown. He also wore a shawl across his chest passing over his left shoulder. He held in his right hand a staff which had a small green colored sphere with the following symbol on it:

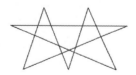

There was one thing characteristic about him. His eyes were chatoyant.

With amazement I said, "Who might you be, Sir?"

"Well you don't need to know my name now. But first, your deduction from the turn of events is absolutely correct. The Giants are still alive."

He continued, "Just tell me what you would do with the treasure if you get it?"

"Well, bring it back to Fymland", said Jason. Meanwhile Mr. Thomas was quiet and serious. He did not speak a word. Seeing Mr. Thomas like that gave me a shiver. Mr. Thomas had never been short of words.

"Well your journey will decide all that", said the mysterious man laughing.

"What journey are you talking about?" Jack asked the mysterious man. The man said nothing.

"So where do we go now to continue our journey? We are sort of blocked underground." Jason continued trying to make him speak.

"First of all you should take this. You will need this. You can use it only once, so use it wisely." Just then a small golden colored sphere shimmered into existence on his hand. I held out my hand and the sphere was passed to me.

"But where do we go and what journey are you talking about?"

"You'll know it sooner than later. Now get going."

Trying to go back the same way we had come, we turned to go but we were dazed to find that the opening through which we entered was now a solid wall.

"You must go through here," pointed the white robed man. We turned and found the opening on the other side.

"Well, I am sure that the opening had been in the opposite direction," said Jack who was dumbfounded.

"That was the entry and now this is the exit." The frail-looking man said curtly. Out of magic or something else, I don't know, Jack was lifted into air and was put straight through the opening.

Just as when I was going to exit the cavern I asked the old man, "Can I know your name now, Sir?"

"You will know that soon when we meet again.

One more thing, you don't need to hold that sphere in your hand all the time. Just wish that it comes to your hand when you want it and wish it to vanish when you do not want it," the magician said smiling and vanished into thin air.

I executed his suggestion finding great difficulty in succeeding. It required a great amount of concentration for the magic to work. Somehow, the golden sphere vanished. Free of encumbrance I exited the cavern. This was my first encounter with magic.

"I hope this takes us back to the fort," I said pointing to the exit.

CHAPTER 7

A tour

On the other side of the exit was a completely different world. I had thought that we would enter into another underground conduit of darkness. But I was wrong. We had walked into a busy, noisy, crowded market. Vegetables and fruit shops stretched on either side of the road. The crowd there seemed to take no notice of us. It was as if they had seen us coming to the market from our houses. But we felt as if we had passed through a portal and not a tunnel exit.

The market was a junction of a variety of people. A shopkeeper from whom I bought an apple was I thought a very bizarre person. He had the body of a muscular man and the face of an innocent man. The peculiar thing about him was that in spite of having an innocent face his voice was so hoarse that immediately after the purchase I ran away from him. "Buy these delicious bananas, only for five cares[1]", he kept shouting in his

---

1   Cares - The currency of Fymland.

croaky voice in an evocative tone. So we were still in Fymland.

Mr. Thomas was the last one to enter the market. He was back to his normal state again. He was as jovial as he was before. I remembered how Mr. Thomas was in the cavern: grave, silent. It felt a bit odd to me. But I postponed the pondering for a later time.

I could make out from the look on his face that he too was perplexed like us but was somehow cheery. Just as he stepped out, the exit compressed itself into a very small point and then it was gone; gone from this reality of life. Being forced by all teachers to read books, I thought them uninteresting but now they had helped me to realize the truth. I said, "This was actually a portal! Not an exit." It was pretty epiphany. Magic was something I believed happened only in fairy tales.

"So where are we?" asked Mr. Thomas.

"We are in a busy, noisy and a crowded market," said Jason.

"Let's try heading straight and see if we could find something useful," said Jack.

We headed straight; meanwhile I had my personal thoughts. Almost my whole childhood had been spent in the Flareds, and yet I hated it. I didn't know who my parents where, I didn't know why they left me in the orphanage and I was pretty angry at them for this.

But now, I more or less missed my orphanage. How much ever Mrs. Philips would torture me, I realized that Flareds had not been as bad as it seemed to be. I missed the fun I had with my friends in our room. But now my life had turned upside down. I had started on a quest with my friends and an eccentric and unpredictable teacher. A quest that could get us crushed by the Giants, viz if they still existed as pronounced by the magician. Abruptly, I realized that we had all ended up in a world full of magic. This was like a fairy tale. Sure this was an adventure but now I realized that living a simple life was much better.

But when I look at it from the other way I realized that this adventure is not as wasteful as it seemed earlier. What if we would end up finding out the great treasure and the famous ruby of Ganohan? Who knows? This adventure would not be a waste after all.

Coming out of my thoughts I looked around to get my bearings. I still wondered where we were. True, we were in a noisy market but where was this market? I asked my friends, "Where is this place?"

"We don't know that," said Jack.

"I hope that we are still in Fymland."

"Oh! Don't worry we are still in Fymland," said Jason.

"Oh my God!" said Mr. Thomas, "There is one problem; we are in the Upper Valley."

"Upper Valley? How can you say that?" I asked.

"Because I am looking right at the 'Famous restaurant of the upper valley,'" Mr. Thomas said.

"That means we have walked for seventy miles without a break?" Jack said who was amazed by Mr. Thomas's reply.

"Well that was partly magic. The exit through which we came here was a portal that transferred us from the lower valley to the upper valley," I said.

"Who was that strange man?" asked Jason.

"He was sort of a magician, I think" Jack paused and then continued, "With that long beard and the staff in his hand, he more or less looked like a magician."

"This expedition is turning out to be interesting," said Jason.

"Well I don't know about that. All I know is that I am very hungry right now," said Jack moving his hand over his stomach as a gesture of hunger.

"Do you still have your wallet Mr. Thomas?" asked Jason.

"Yes I do have it. But Why?" he asked.

On understanding the whole plan I said, "Well then, you've got to give us a treat."

The food in the restaurant turned out to be quite good as suggested by the passers- by. My stomach was full. "So where do we go now?" I asked others.

"Let's try finding that mysterious man," Jack suggested.

"He had said that he would meet us soon. So why bother to find him?" I said.

"Okay then let's meet him as and when it happens," said Jason.

It had almost been an hour since we left the restaurant. The market was long behind us now. Houses with stucco walls stretched on either side of the street.

They varied in size and color. The bucolic atmosphere conflated superbly with stucco houses.

At one spot beside the street was an open place where a bench lay. I went and sat there, followed by others. Bemoaning, I said, "Finding this old man is like catching a mirage. Oh Dane! We are getting a tour of the Upper Valley. Will someone tell me which is the right place to find this magician?"

"Just opposite the street," said Mr. Thomas.

"How did you know?" asked Jack.

"Because I am now looking right at it across the street," said Jason.

CHAPTER 8

History Lesson

I followed Mr. Thomas's gaze. He was looking at a nameless, antique shop. It was comparatively smaller than the others beside it. It had black curtains instead of a door for the entrance. I thought that the weird man had no sense of security. But what caught my eye was that the banner showing the shop name had the picture of the same green colored sphere which was on the magician's staff.

We crossed the street and reached shop. Crossing the street required some skill and effort. The market was far behind but the noise was still loud. There, in the market, it was due to the sales pitch of the shopkeepers and here it is due to the honking of cars. It took us a while to get to the other side of the street.

As soon as we entered the shop the noise stopped. No sounds could be heard inside the shop. It was as if we had entered a different world. I turned round. There was not even a single car on the street. "What's wrong with that curtain?" asked Jack.

"Let's find out," said Jason. He reached out for the curtain but suddenly stopped halfway. He drew back his hand and tried again but again he stopped. It looked as if an invisible barrier had blocked the movement of his hand.

"What happened Jason?" I asked

"Something is blocking my hand."

"Magic again! It may be an invisible barrier."

"Yeah, it may be."

"So this man lives in a protected world," I thought.

"Yes I do!" said the image of the magician that popped up on the curtain. He looked a bit angry which I thought, was partly due to our constant banter.

The image showed only his upper body and the green sphere of his staff. He said challengingly, "Show me that you all are worthy of entering my abode."

"So what now?" Jason asked.

"I think you should show him the sphere that he gave you," said Mr. Thomas.

"Okay but…," I stammered.

"But what?" Jack asked.

"There's one problem. He said that I can use this sphere only once."

"Come on Alex. You are not using it. You are just showing it to him," Mr. Thomas said.

"Okay."

I wished for the golden sphere to appear in my hand but nothing happened. I concentrated and tried once again and this time it appeared in my hand. I lifted it up in the air so that it was visible to the face on the screen.

I said, "This is the sphere that you gave me. You said that it would help me. I am able to deploy it whenever I wish to. Can we now enter?"

"Well okay." On saying that, the curtain was automatically drawn and we entered.

Inside his house was nothing but empty space. No furniture, no place to sit, nothing. Ahead, stood the magician smiling. "Welcome," he said.

"So, can I know your name now? I asked.

"Yes, I am Glore and I belong nowhere. I am a magician and a scientist and travel round the world. Today, you are going to have a history lesson. Sit down."

"What do we sit on?" asked Jason.

"On the floor," replied the magician.

As we tried to sit there appeared stone chairs out of thin air.

"Long ago in a cave in the Egor Mountains ...." began the magician.

"Where's that?" interrupted Jack.

"It's a place somewhere. I know that Fymland is the world for you all but it's nothing compared to the world outside. Please do not interrupt again. Fifty one years ago in a cave in the Egor Mountains, the great blacksmiths of Iregor gathered to forge the most powerful weapon of the world – The Ruby of Ganohan. I know it's strange. A ruby is a precious stone but this ruby is much more than that, it is a weapon of mass destruction. It can destroy a whole army with a single blow. The blacksmiths spent a year in the cave working hard every day to forge the ruby. When Maut, the Giant king whose power was equal to that of one hundred elephants, came to know about it he immediately led an army to Iregor. The Iregorians were helpless. The end result, Maut grabbed the ruby from the Iregorians and fixed it on his scepter. He conquered the whole world using the ruby. Nothing could withstand its power, not even the finest blade. It radiated pure evil. But your Fymland was more or less safe due to the four lords. The four lords namely Roalf, the lord of wind, Sior, the lord of Earth, Leon, the lord of fire and the most powerful of them all, Dane, the lord of water." I gasped.

He continued, "One day the lords met in Sumter Fort to decide the fate of the ruby of Ganohan. They decided that the ruby had to be destroyed at any cost. But they didn't know how to destroy it. Leon proposed that they would make Maut himself do that. So the Lords with their armies gathered on the grounds of Gorum for the biggest battle with Giants. The Lords realized that defeating the Giants was impossible for them. They had to somehow distract Maut to be able to wean the ruby from him. They together attacked and killed the son of Maut. When Maut was busy shedding tears for his Giant son, the lords took away his scepter and dislodged the ruby. But the power of the ruby was so immense that it sucked the souls out of Lords Sior and Leon who were holding the scepter. Luckily, as Lords Dane and Roalf were at a distance keeping an eye on King Maut their souls were saved. To prevent the radiation from the ruby hitting them, they covered it with their armor and escaped to Fymland, Dane's dominion, with the ruby and the treasure of Ganohan. The people of Fymland did not know the powers of the ruby. So Dane told them that the ruby was a part of the treasure. That's why you must have heard a completely different legend.

But the curse of the ruby had befallen on the surviving Lords. Nothing could prevent this catastrophe from happening. This had cost Dane his life and you know that as The Last Battle of Dane. His opposition was not only Maut but also the Lords Sior and Leon who had become slaves of Giant King Maut because of the ruby. Every soul that the ruby sucked in would bow to the commands of Maut.

Dane protected Fymland till his last breath by fighting the battle on the Western Borders. When he died the free soul of Dane liberated the souls of Lords Sior and Leon from the ruby as their spirits were interconnected at the elemental level. Dane wished Roalf - The Lord of Wind did not fight the Giants alone as he was needed to stay alive to take care of their progeny and ready a new army for a fresh battle with the Giants at a later time.

The Giants returned to Ganohan with the ruby and the treasure without hurting the people of Fymland. No one knows the reason for this behavior of the Giants. You could ask your geography teacher about that." Glore chuckled saying that and continued: "By the way Mr. Thomas, your geography teacher here, is the Lord of Wind – Roalf."

His words shocked us. Our geography teacher, Mr. Thomas was Roalf? He was just a teacher at the Flareds. How could he be Roalf? I looked at him... he was very somber. All the time during the lecture I had been watching him. He was not paying much attention. He was nonchalant and gesturing as if he knew the whole story. But now that he was paying attention, I asked Glore, "If Mr. Thomas is Roalf then he should have at least been born seventy five years ago. But Mr. Thomas is just a young man of age thirty who knows nothing about wars and battles."

The answer that came shocked us even more. "Well he's kind of immortal and is not a young man at all, given his age." Glore laughed out loud saying this.

"What!" I, Jack and Jason cried in unison. It was disturbing to know that Mr. Thomas was Roalf and that he is immortal.

Meanwhile Mr. Thomas said, "Are you sure Glore?"

"Yes I am, Roalf; the time has come to tell them the truth about themselves."

"But they are just children."

"Yes they are. But it will be too late if we delay."

"Wait a minute. Who is Roalf?" interrupted Jason amusingly.

"I am", said Mr. Thomas without a smile on his face. He continued, "Yes I am Roalf, the Lord of wind. Do you want to know the reason for that strange behavior of the Giants and why I was so desperate for this adventure and that too with you kids? Here it is. Just before the grand meeting of Dane, Sior and Leon, their three children were born who would sooner or later become the new Lords. Their names were Jack, son of Sior, Jason, son of Leon, and Alex, son of Dane."

A chill ran down our backs. Until now, I had not believed in any legend or story about Dane. But today I get to know that I am the son of the father whom I believed did not exist. I showed an expressionless face but hid an enormous guilt. I looked at Jack and Jason. They held the same expressionless face as mine.

Roalf continued, "But you were all just a year old then. For your safety they put you all in Sumter Fort. At the end of the war when King Dane was about to die, he extracted an oath from me to keep you all safe and to destroy the ruby at an opportune time. Bounded by this promise I could not wage a war alone against the Giants. He handed this task to me because I was the only surviving Lord. When I was protecting you all in Sumter Fort, the Giants found us. I enclosed all of you in a shell to protect you. Maut tried to kill you all but I worked a gust of wind that swept you all miles away from Fymland. But I could not help to keep the ruby safe as it had already formed the part of his scepter after the defeat of King Dane. The ruby had found its master again. When you were grown up enough to get education, I put you in the Flareds Academy and I got myself employed there as a geography teacher. Since then I have been protecting you all. In short, you three are the descendants of the Lords."

CHAPTER 9

The Start of Adventure

Whoever Mr. Thomas was, it was very hard to believe the truth. Something in my mind was continuously forcing me to disbelieve this. It told me that this Glore was just creating a new mythology. But still, even this was hard to accept. I could not choose between either.

"As if reading my thoughts, Glore said, "The truth is always the truth. It is sometimes hard to accept it but you have to. Have you ever wondered why you kids liked history lessons that were about battles and wars? It's because it is in your brethren to fight and slay. You three were born to fight and destroy evil. Why would Mr. Thomas go on this adventure with you three?"

"Yes" said Roalf rashly, "why would I go on this adventure with only three puny little children who are afraid to realize their own powers?" This sarcasm hit us hard.

We said in unison, "Roalf, we trust you." He calmed down a bit as we chose to accept the truth and follow our collective destiny.

Roalf said jovially, "How old are you guys?"

"Sixteen," I said.

"No you're not. Who told you that?" Roalf asked.

"Both Mrs. Philips and the director of Flareds." I answered.

"Did someone else say? Did I?" He asked. I didn't reply. He continued, "Lords take time to grow at the start. A sixteen year old lord is the size of a five year old normal child, maybe even less than that."

"I don't believe this," Jack said.

"Yeah this is rubbish," Jason agreed.

"No it's not," Roalf said as a matter of factly.

Jason asked, "Were the Lords, Gods with all those powers?"

Glore said, "They were not Gods to be worshipped. Remember people did not worship them. But yes, they had powers."

Jack asked, "Do we have powers too?"

"Of course you have, but you have to realize it and learn to control it yourself. No one can help you with that. Roalf can suggest you a bit." I was taken aback by his answer. I didn't want any powers. It was exciting to know. It makes you feel that you're strongest in the world and that you can rise above the common. Nonetheless I wanted to be a normal kid. But I knew we had no choice.

"Can we begin now?" I asked.

"What?" asked Roalf.

"This adventure of course, waging war, destroying the ruby...," I said.

"There is time for all that kid. Get some rest now. I can see that you are all exhausted. Tonight we rest, and tomorrow we start at eight," said Roalf.

"But where do we sleep. There is no bed and enough space for all of us here," Jack said.

"Oh! I just forgot about that," Glore said, "What you see is just an illusion. Focus and look closely." We looked closely but all we could see was the small bounded space that we were in.

But Jason said, "What kind of a trick is this? I can see only the four walls of this room."

"You are not looking hard. Concentrate, Focus." Glore said, "This is magic. And in your adventure you're going to encounter more of such illusions. So just concentrate. Imagine that this is the beginning of your training." We all concentrated once again. We closed our eyes for a while to boost our concentration and then opened eyes and looked hard. From somewhere smoke rose but it had no smell. I waved my hand in an effort to clear the smoke but could touch nothing. The smoke did not hurt our eyes. After a while the smoke cleared and a big room with five beds appeared. When the smoke fully cleared we all could see clearly a room that was far better than the ones at Flareds.

The room was so big that it appeared to have an endless floor with the apparition of walls and ceiling at a height. I told myself to get used to this world of magic. I could see a blue wall with a bed abutting it at the far corner. I turned right and could see a green wall with a bed lying alongside. I again turned right and could see an orange – red wall with a bed next to it. I turned right and could see the same pattern except the wall grayish – white. And in the centre of the whole room was a single bed that was the biggest of all.

"There's not much of difference between this room and that of the illusion. That was small one with plenty of empty space and this one is a big room which accommodates only five beds", I said as a matter of factly.

"Yeah, that's true," Jack and Jason said in unison. Which meant even they had been successful in the so called 'test of magic'.

Ignoring my comment Glore said, "Remember both the rooms are an illusion; nothing is real. I think you may have understood by now that the power of illusion is of great value. And now, the bed abutting the blue wall is for Alex; the one at the grey wall is for Roalf; the one at the red wall is for Jason; and the one at the green wall is for Jack."

"And the one in the center?" I asked.

"That's for me of course! I am going to be with you all tonight," came the answer from Glore.

"Do we get anything to eat or sleep with an empty stomach?" Jack asked.

"You'll not get any food but just a glass of juice," saying that Glore held out his hand. A tray with four glasses of juice appeared on his hand. Each of us excluding Glore took a glass. After drinking it I immediately felt drowsy. Jason asked, "Did you mix a sleeping pill in that juice, I'm feeling drowsy."

"Yeah, more or less a sleeping pill. Now off to sleep, all of you," Glore said.

I went and collapsed on my bed. The very next minute I was snoring like a monster. I had a quite peaceful, dreamless sleep. When I woke up, I wondered where I was. I could see Jack and Jason packing their bags. Next to them was Mr. Thomas and an unidentified man. Then suddenly everything flashed in my mind and I remembered how we reached the upper valley and into this house of Glore's. I got up and heard Mr. Thomas's voice, "Hurry up Alex, we are getting late".

Beside my bed was a new door which I was sure did not exist last night. I opened it and found out that it was a bathroom. I finished my morning ablutions as quickly as I could. After that we quickly had our breakfast. Our diet included nothing but bread and butter and a few fruits. Instead of water we had been given juice (it gave energy, Glore said). I had asked Glore about its contents twice before drinking it.

"So where do we go now?" Jack asked after we finished our breakfast.

"Into the portal," saying that, Glore created a portal that radiated a brown colored light just by a wave of his hand. He further continued, "And this map will help you. In order to go to Ganohan, you have to first go to Iregor, where you might or might not receive help." He handed out a map to Jason which looked very old. "This map will lead you to the sacred place of Iregor. Grab some weapons now." He held out his hand and two differently shaped weapons appeared in his hand.

"This one's for you Jack: The Giant Slayer. It was the weapon of Sior." The weapon looked like an Axe but it was much bigger.

"Thanks. But what do you mean by 'might or might not receive help'?" asked Jack. Glore ignored him and Jack went into the portal holding the big axe in his hand.

"This one's for you Jason, the spear of Leon. It's called The Fire Knight."

"Thanks." Taking the spear Jason entered the portal. And after him went Mr. Thomas.

I was the last one. I said, "Glore, I trust you and that's why I'm telling you this. I'm a bit worried. If the ruby is so powerful how can we stop it from spreading its evil? There is no weapon which can do that."

"Who said that there is no weapon which can do that?"

"You mean there is one?" I asked anxiously.

"Of course there is one." He held out both his hands and there appeared a long sword with a sharp blade. It radiated a slight blue hue. It had a small ruby rooted in the blade just above the hilt. "This is the Holy Sword of Iregor. It was forged by the blacksmiths of Iregor in the Cave of Egor Mountains. Always remember when evil is born, good is also born. This sword has the power to destroy the ruby." Saying that he gave the sword to me and when I touched it the slight blue hue became brighter, it was almost sparkling. "Water", I thought. On holding it a new strength flowed into me and I felt stronger than ever before.

"You don't need to carry that in your hands. Keep it in its sheath." He took the sword from me and produced a sheath and in a swift motion kept the sword in its Sheath. It then suddenly vanished and then reappeared on the right side of my pants. It felt much lighter now. But I bet it was because of the magic of the sheath. I felt much more confident as the sword hung on my side.

Glore continued, "I know you still are a little scared. Your friends feel the same. They are just not showing it. You just need a push. Tell me why would Dane on his deathbed ask Roalf to protect you all and to help you destroy the ruby?"

"I don't know," I said.

"Because Dane had died believing in a world free of Evil...at least for a while. Even Dane had been scared when he had to fight that great battle with the Giants. But yet he moved on because he was destined for it. I don't want to compare, but like Dane even you are the strongest among the four. You were born for it. Only you can destroy the ruby. Yes, you are destined for it. Do you know why Dane was the strongest? Because of his element, Water. This beautiful world that we see today would have been incomplete without water. There would have been no life on Earth but for water."

"But water doesn't exist everywhere on Earth like Wind. How can I use my power?" I asked.

"You don't need a river or a sea to use your power. This is a world where illusion prevails, a world where dreams come true; a world where your imaginations make you the strongest. Magic is like a comely bungalow in the middle of an oasis. Magic is ethereal and evanescent. Farewell to you. I hope we meet again. Good Luck."

I was not scared now. My blood flowed with confidence. I felt ebullience in my gut. "Thanks Glore." With those last words I entered the portal with the single aim in my mind: The destruction of the Ruby of Ganohan. Our Adventure had begun.

CHAPTER 10

A little rest

On the other side of the portal stood Roalf, Jack and Jason. I looked at the surroundings. There was greenery everywhere. Trees rose about 30 meters high above the ground. The canopy formed by the trees blocked the sunlight making it very dark. We had landed up in the middle of a forest.

The portal closed behind us. I approached my friends. They were focusing on the map that Glore had given us. It was glowing in the dark. "Where are we?"

"Look at the map," said Roalf. I did as he said. At the bottom of the map was a script that read "You are here". That script was written in the centre of something that looked like a cloud. The cloud was named "Egilium Forests".

Surprised, I asked, "How is it that we are in the Egilium Forests?"

"I know it's strange, but the map says it is." Jason said.

"I thought the Egilium Forests were small."

"We are seeing how small these are," Roalf said.

"Hold on," I said, "if these are the Egilium Forests then the Egil River has to be somewhere here, I pointed to a location on the map."

"But we are not seeing it here", said Jack.

"Come on guys, you have to get used to this strange world. This is our world." Roalf said calmly. This made me angry.

I said, "I know you're the Great Lord of Wind. We were brought into this surreal world by you against our wishes. We could walk all the way back to Fymland if we wished."

"Of course, Alex you could but the problem is that you don't know the way back. Look Alex," He held my shoulders and said, "I don't know what you think of this ruby and the Giants, but this is a serious matter. If we don't stop Maut now then we all could get killed; and that will be against your own wish!" He stressed a bit on the last four words.

I calmed down and said, "I guess we should go straight."

"Yes, that's what's in the map," Jason said. Ahead of us stretched a narrow road that led to a place we didn't know. It was the only road that we saw. Everything else beside it was covered with trees.

"Let's make our way then," Jack said. I admit it; he looked more confident and bolder than me and Jason. It was due to his element - Earth, I guessed. Earth was around us everywhere.

Our walk through the forest was not very interesting. The road was so narrow and undulating that it was impossible for us to walk side by side. It was more like a march than a leisure walk. Trees stretched on either side of us. The roots created obstacles in our path. Many a time, I stumbled. I looked at Jack. There was no difference in his confidence. Not even once did he stumble.

Suddenly Jason said, "I do not understand - if Roalf is really the Lord of Wind then he should know the way to Iregor. Why do we need a map then?"

"That's a good question," I said.

Roalf rubbed his hair and said; "It has been years since the battle of Sumter Fort. Since then I'm in Fymland. I've actually forgotten the route."

"A very good excuse," Jack said laughing.

Unexpectedly an idea struck me. I asked Jack, "Jack, you are the son of Sior, the Lord of Earth. Glore said that we have some powers. So can you get some of these trees off our path so that we could get more space to walk faster?"

"Good thinking," Roalf said.

Then Jack answered, "But I wouldn't do that. Why should we disturb the ecosystem of this place?" This answer was annoying but Jack was right. Disturbing the ecosystem was certainly wrong. So we rambled on.

After a while there was a clearing in the forest and the road widened. It was enough for us to walk in a group now. Presently the sunlight could reach the ground. Jason who was very tired went under the shade of the nearest tree and sat down on the smooth grass. The rest of the party followed him and sat down. Every one of us including Roalf was hungry and the gastronomic juices were slowly getting released in our stomachs.

Hungry? Roalf asked Jack, "What's the time by your watch, Jack."

"I'm sorry Roalf. My watch is not working," said Jack.

Roalf looked at me and Jason expecting an answer but didn't get any as we had no watches. He looked at the Sun. It was high up in the sky. "I guess its afternoon. Let's have our lunch." We kept our weapons aside. Jack, Jason and Roalf had not known which weapon Glore had given me and I did not intend to tell them. Till now I had not seen Roalf having any weapon.

Jack, who had the bag with food supplies, brought out sandwiches which did not look that good. However, we did not have a choice. So we ate them.

While Jason and Jack were lost in eating their sandwiches, I heard Roalf say, "It seems you had a good talk with Glore."

"Yeah, he somehow managed to convince me," I said.

"You had to be convinced. This quest cannot be successful without you. We are incomplete without the Lord of Water."

"Okay, thanks, but please stop that 'Lord' thing."

"What weapon did Glore give you? I can see that he has given you a sword."

"He has given me the holy sword of Iregor."

"What's that?"

"You don't know that?" I was baffled, "It was made at the same time as the ruby. He said that it has the power to destroy it."

"Oh! Good. But I've never heard anything about such a sword."

I was bowled over by his answer. How could Roalf, the Lord of wind who had fought the great battle, not know about the Holy Sword? Then the next second, everything fell into place. If the Holy Sword had been used in the Great War then the ruby would have been destroyed long ago. But the previous Lords did not know about its existence. And that's the reason why Roalf knew nothing about it.

The sandwiches were not sumptuous but they were just alright. We finished our lunch quickly. Jason wanted to take a nap but Roalf did not let him sleep.

There were no other people in the forest. It was as quite as it could get. I felt very forlorn although I had my friends with me. Then abruptly Jack broke the silence, "I've discovered that my axe can vanish and reappear as per my wish."

I hadn't seen Jack losing his axe before. "Can you show us?" Roalf asked.

Jack closed his eyes and concentrated. He moved his eyebrows. I could see that he was stressing. And then all of a sudden, the axe appeared in his hands. He repeated the same thing again and the axe disappeared. "It takes a lot out of me to do this," he said.

"You'll get used to it. But for now it's very good."

"Very good Jack," I said patting his back.

Then Jason said, "I want to try."

"Show us what you can do but don't copy Jack, be creative," Mr. Thomas said.

"Okay", saying that he held his spear, closed his eyes and concentrated. The spear resized itself. It had become small. "Whoa, I made it into a walking stick." We sat back and laughed loudly. The lonely feeling was escaping my heart. I felt much better.

"You truly are an old man!" Roalf said laughing.

"But not as old as you." At this we laughed even louder.

"Anyways, what did Glore give to you, Alex?" Jack asked.

All of a sudden I stopped laughing. I wasn't sure about telling them about the holy sword. I hesitated to answer. Then I finally made up my mind to tell them, "He gave me the Holy Sword of Iregor."

"What's that?" Jason asked.

"This", saying that I removed my sword from its sheath. The sword glimmered even in sunlight. Its length and sharpness could send a shiver down any soldier at war; but may not be the Giants as they are beasts without fear. The sword's hilt gave me a superb grip. I felt a sudden pulse of energy and courage ripple through my whole body.

Astonished, Jack said, "What a sword!"

"Yeah Jack," Jason said, "It can make a deep cut even by a slight touch."

"It's truly holy. Only Iregorians can forge such a sword. What you were saying was true Alex," Roalf said.

"Yeah. This sword has the power to destroy the ruby," I said.

"But to destroy it we have to reach Ganohan. Let's continue our journey then." Roalf said.

I got up and put the sword back into its sheath and hung it on the side of my waist. We returned to the road and continued our journey with brave hearts. Fear had left us long ago. With weapons concealed, we moved on.

CHAPTER 11

We enter the forest where the light ceases

I was a bit surprised by their reaction when I showed them my sword. I thought that they would crave to handle the sword but they didn't. They were happy for me to have been gifted the Sword of Iregor by Glore and were eagerly looking forward to serve the purpose of our quest. They were just like their fathers Sior and Leon in character and spirit.

We continued our journey through the Egilium Forests on the rough terrain. Nothing had changed about the road except that it had widened allowing us to walk side by side. Jack and Jason were playing with their weapons, Roalf kept brushing his long hair and I simply walked watching them affectionately. I felt a sense of purpose with the sword at my side. I realized that it was a storehouse of energy and I could access it freely. No doubt it will help me slay the Giants and destroy the ruby. But presently I was feeling a bit uneasy for reasons that I could not guess.

I looked up at the sky. It was cloudless with the Sun shining like a ball of fire. Fire, I thought about Jason, the son of Leon and the Lord of Fire. He was a kind of person whose face would not give any hint of his thoughts or his confidence level. But certainly I felt he was getting used to the new situation. We had all more or less accepted our new roles.

It was a pleasant afternoon. Grass stretched on either side of the road. There was a scent of rosemary in the air. In the distance I could see the existence of a cave which was covered by green leaves.

Then I heard Jason say, "What about you Roalf?"

"Can you be more specific?" came the answer.

"Don't you have any weapon?"

"Yes I do have one, but you don't need to see it now. I am quite good without my weapon."

"But we want to see it now," Jack said eagerly.

"Don't worry, you'll see it soon when we are attacked by Giants," Roalf said.

"What! Are we going to be attacked in this quiet and lonely forest?" Jason asked worriedly.

'Why, are you scared? You think this is a lonely forest? You are wrong. There might be spies peering on us even as we talk now."

I looked at the surroundings but I caught no sign of any spy. But what if he was right? Maybe that was why I was feeling uneasy. But I still couldn't believe the fact that there were spies looking at us this very second because they would be seen easily in this clearing. We were still in the clearing which was very big.

"What are you looking around for? They are spies… and well trained ones."

Okay… calm down – I told my worried heart - There is no reason to worry about. You're the Lord of Water and the son of the most powerful man that was on this Earth. Even if the spies see you, they won't hurt you because you have your lord friends by your side. "So don't worry," I told myself. This was enough to console my heart.

There was no conversation for a while. Jack was walking the fastest. He was taking such long steps that were not befitting his height. Jack was a short person. Jason, as always, held an expressionless face. So I could make out nothing. He was weighing on his spear, which he had turned into a walking stick, every time he took a step.

Roalf, the Lord of Wind was waving his hand in the air as if he was trying to feel and control the wind. He looked as if this adventure was just a minor riddle to solve. But it was not the same for the rest of us.

I looked around and slowed down my pace and lay my hand on the sword butt, ready to unsheathe it if the need arises.

The cave in the distance could be now seen more clearly. Wait…something was different…it did not look like a cave.

"Is that a cave in the distance?" I asked perplexed.

"I don't think so." Jack answered. He held the same perplexed face as I did.

"Let's find out what it actually is," Roalf volunteered.

We ran towards the cave or whatever it might be. Reaching it I realized my mistake. The thing that looked like a cave covered with leaves was a thick canopy formed by the short trees. My friends looked at it in astonishment and I was no different. I had never seen an awning so thick and at such a low level. Beyond it stretched a dark forest which instantly gave me goose bumps. Regardless of whether or not humans can smell fear, they can certainly hear it and I heard it in Jason's voice.

"So what shall we do now?" Jason asked.

"We'll have to enter, there's no other choice," Roalf answered with supreme confidence. He was the man who 'has seen it' and 'done it all' in the past.

"It's looking very scary," Jack said. He still had his elemental confidence which was also boosted partly because of Roalf's answer.

"I completely agree with you Jack!" I said.

"We can't back off now. Let's make our way through it," Roalf decreed and started walking fast.

"Wait a minute. Please check the map as to whether we are onto the right path." I said to Jason. Jason took out the map from his backpack and we all at once peered into it. Going through the forest was the only way to get to Iregor – as shown in the map. This was the Bulkite Forest.

"The word in the local language of Iregor means, 'The forest where the light ceases'." Roalf told me. Yes, I agree, the name is pretty frightening. Having no other choice, we had to enter the forest.

Roalf looked up at the sky for the last time. "It looks like it's five o' clock now. We have three hours to get as far as we can in the forest. At eight we will have dinner and after that we'll rest."

I turned back and could see the sunrays falling on the smooth meadow. I could see the pacifying shade of the tree under which we had rested. It felt more and more appealing. However, purposefully I turned back and entered the forest where the light ceased.

CHAPTER 12

In the Forest

The sight of the inside of the forest gave me a shiver. The outskirts of the forest were not so dark but I could see absolutely nothing in the distance. Behind me, I could see the bright day light, which in the interior of the forest was slowly fading as we progressed.

I looked up at the canopy which was very thick, but I knew that the canopies in the interior would be much thicker. There were scarcely any sun rays that could make their way in from the top. But the ones that did could not bring enough light to our path. "We have to stay focused," Roalf said.

The trees, as far as my eye sight in dim light could go, were a flush of deep green and their barks were deep brown. The trees were lined with shrubs so large that they almost covered the only pathway. The feel of the ground was that of crumpled leaves and some hard, broad curved structures which I guessed to be the tree roots.

There was a smell of wet soil in the air, so naturally I was excited. As we walked the light was slowly fading and after a few minutes we came to a place where it was completely dark. I carefully turned to look at the fading light. Well, all I could see was a single speck of brightness.

"Friends?" I called out into the darkness.

"We are near you," the answer came in unison.

"Let's hold our hands," I suggested. After holding hands I realized that Jason and Roalf were right beside me and Jack likewise.

"I need some light," Jack said.

"Jason can you make some fire?" I asked.

"That would be too bright. Alex, can you unsheathe your sword; we have seen that it has a blue-watery glow," said Jack.

"No, not Alex. I will tell you why later. Let Jason create the ball of fire in his hand." Roalf said.

Jason concentrated. I could feel it as he seized my hand tightly. This was the first time he was going to show his elemental power. We were all excited. I hoped that he will achieve success. He held out his right hand as I felt some upheaval pass through him. First try was in vain. His second try was successful. The fire came to life as his body relaxed. The flames danced on his hands vigorously. I could see his face now and there was no hint of pain. Roalf told him to make the fire dimmer and doing this was easy for Jason as he succeeded in one go.

I could see everybody now, even the surroundings. The flames of Jason's fire danced on every one's face. So it looked as if our faces were continuously changing their hue and structure.

We started walking once again and Roalf started explaining:

"There are two basic energies in the world – Positive and negative. Alex's sword contains a lot of positive energy. I can sense it. And the giants are made up of only negative energy. Positive attracts negative."

"Yeah, we have learned that in Physics," Jack said

"Yes. So whenever the giants come near a source of positive energy, they are attracted towards it. As we don't know these surroundings presently we have to be cautious. The meadow back there was the last safe area and now we have entered a zone of perils and dangers. And from now on we speak quietly. Understood?"

"Yes." We, the students, said in unison.

Roalf's explanation lingered in my mind for a long time. It made me realize that I was in peril all the time. I was completely engrossed in his explanation without any doubt. The fact that my sword contained positive energy scared me. It meant that whenever I was near any giant it would be very difficult for me to escape just because that giant would get attracted to me. However, I cast these thoughts out of my mind and listened to what Roalf was saying:

"Let's camp here tonight, we start early in the morning. We keep watch one by one."

We gathered some fallen branches and leaves by stretching out our hands in the darkness. Jason lighted them. Then we rested against a huge tree that was just beside us visible in the fire light. Jason was the first one to keep the watch followed by Jack and then me and then Roalf. It was easy to fall asleep after walking continuously for three hours and covering a large distance. Gradually, I drew back from reality and fell into my own slumber.

"Wake up, Alex, wake up!"

I slowly opened my eyes…I had a blurred vision. Above me I could see a small rectangular face with high cheek bones. The eyebrows were raised up and wrinkles were visible on the forehead. A second later I could clearly see the anxious face of Jason with fire in his hand. I got up with a start and nearly made Jason fall down.

"What happened?" I asked.

"Talk softly," Roalf whispered.

"I can sense some movement nearby but we are at a safe distance from it. I can feel it moving in our direction." Jack said.

"So what do we do?"

"Since we can go nowhere in this forest, we have no other choice but to climb this tree." Jason said pointing towards the tree under which we were resting.

This was not a good idea. It made me hesitate but I couldn't help it. I had never ever climbed a tree in my life. I had only seen coconut vendors climbing and cutting the coconuts from the tall coconut trees found in the lower valley of Fymland. I remembered their technique of climbing the trees.

Jason put out the campfire. We could see the surroundings with the help of the fire on his hand. Jack was the first to climb. It was naturally easy for him to do so. I studied him closely while he was climbing. Next to go up was me. I came to the tree and spread my arms round it. I put my right leg on the tree and then giving myself an upward push I put the left leg on the tree at a higher elevation. I continued to climb the tree in this way. I was slow but managed to climb without falling to the ground. My sword hung on the side of my waist. It did not bother me while I was climbing the tree which I knew was due to the magic of the sheath. I had developed an emotional bond with it during our journey. My sword was the one that gave me confidence to continue with this adventure.

On reaching the top I found that there was enough space for me to sit on one of the thick branches. Jack had already found one for himself. Next came Jason and found himself a branch above mine.

"Where's Roalf?" I asked.

"Look up." The answer came. I looked up and found Roalf at the highest point of the tree, at the canopy. He must have flown up – I thought. Jason extinguished the fire in his hand making it impossible for us to see.

We waited for some time. After a while I could hear some footsteps.

"They are near. I can sense it." Jack whispered.

"Me too." I said.

"But I think there are two people who are coming towards us," Jason said.

"Yeah, I agree with you, Jason." I said.

"Now listen," Roalf advised.

The footsteps were now louder. I could clearly hear them. They were heavy. I guessed that the creatures that were advancing towards us were huge and could make the ground shake when they walked. I hoped that they were not the Giants. If so, then this would be my first encounter with them. I hoped that they would not be as dangerous as Roalf talked about them.

Then suddenly the noise of the footsteps stopped… they must have come to a halt. Then one of them spoke for the first time which sent a shiver down my spine giving me goose bumps.

CHAPTER 13

Ronkar and Batchels

"Someone had camped here." The voice was very deep and hoarse. His voice box was over working as he spoke.

"I can see that, you fool," the other one said. This man's voice was even croakier than his pal. But how could he see? Maybe they have 'Night Vision'. If it was so then we were in great danger because if he looks up, then…I don't need to complete that. I hoped that his head wouldn't tilt back sufficiently to make him look at us.

I could not see anything in the darkness. It was obvious. I strained my eyes but it was of no use. It's very irritating to see nothing. You see almost everything around you in this world with your good eyes and then darkness covers everything around you and your eyes are of no use then. You can't even close your eyes and take a nap because if you do so you might be any minute sleeping between a pack of hyenas. In such a situation the only sense organ that can help you is your ear. And I was using my hearing power as much as I could.

"It was some human. Yes, Batchels they are nearby. I can smell them." The first one said.

I was feeling increasingly uncomfortable on the single thick branch which bore my weight. There were no thorns on the branch, it was quite smooth. My lower back was paining now. I continuously shifted in my place trying to find some comfortable posture, carefully, without making any noise.

The wind started blowing heavily. I felt it on my face. My senses told me that a storm was approaching. The first hint was the rain. Initially, it poured slowly then heavily. There was a petrichor smell. I felt the thick, broad hardwood leaves of the tree caressing my face gently. They were wet. I too was covered with water but I was not wet because of my ancestry. I was in high spirits now as I came in contact with water on my body for the first time since the start of this adventure.

"This ash here...some human, I'm sure...their flesh...Oh! Ronkar how did we miss it. I'm hungry." Batchels said greedily.

"You only think about food. Grow up, you idiot. We haven't missed them. They are close, very close." Ronkar said coldly.

"Then let's catch them and take them to the master, brother. He must be waiting for some delicious warm – blooded humans." Batchels said.

"Yeah, good, then let's run with the wind and bring doom to the humans who dare to enter master's land," Ronkar laughed with malevolence. They started running around a small distance from the tree. The ground started shaking from the thumping it received from the heavy weight bodies' running. Within no time we could see two huge shapes at a faraway distance running parallel to each other. The shapes were covered with a glow that had a faint tinge of green and blue. Their movements were desultory. After a while the huge shapes turned back and started running in our direction. As they were approaching back toward our tree the contours of the shapes grew clearer.

"Are they Giants?" I whispered loudly.

Roalf said "Quiet!"

A faint smell of garlic was carried by the air as the shapes were approaching us. The Giants had two feet attached to each leg! May be this was required for them to balance their huge bodies. Their skin was twisted all over and looked graphitic. The skin texture looked like scales on a crocodile body.

The Giants had three horns; the middle one being slightly longer than the side ones. Their ears had grown forward making them look like blinkers in a horse tack. We soon realized that the Giants could only see straight ahead like a blinkered horse and not to the sides. Just then I tried hurriedly to adjust my position on the branch on which I was sitting and pushed the front half with my hands to move my body backwards. The push from my hands was a bit too much on the front part of the slender branch and it suddenly broke. I barely had enough time to latch on to the remaining half attached to the tree. But fortunately, the Giants did not hear the cracking of the branch as they were still a distance away. But by the time the branch fell to the ground with a muffled crackle on the wet leaves the Giants had almost reached the tree. This low pitched noise was clearly picked up by the Giants' large ears.

The Giants stopped suddenly in their tracks.

"Oops!" I whispered.

A sudden silence filled the forest and then it was broken by the roaring noise of Ronkar.

"What was that?" he shouted. "Who made that noise? Come out you coward! Don't hide from me. I'll tear you to pieces! Who dares to spy on Ronkar and Batchels, the favorite twin giants of the King of Ganohan?" saying that he began punching the tree on which we were sitting. The tree began shaking heavily. I told myself not to panic. I held the trunk of the tree tightly and closed my eyes.

"Don't look up. Don't look up. Don't look up." I prayed silently. My heart was almost thumping. I could hear it in my ears like a war drum. Beads of sweat travelled down my cheeks quickly. They mixed with the rain water and tasted salty. I felt a sudden stroke of nausea. I tried to control myself. I heard Jack mutter, "Oh my God". Jason and Roalf were quiet all this time.

But soon we realized that the Giants could not move up their heads to the sky because of the twisted scales present on the back of their necks too. This was a real blessing for us.

"Cool down brother," Batchels said, "The noise was just that of a fallen branch."

Ronkar was out of breath and could just say, "Oh!"

"Let's go and catch those puny little creatures later, we have wasted enough time here."

"Yeah let's go. Master must be waiting."

I calmed down a bit as they started moving. Their heavy footsteps echoed through the forest breaking its silence. I could hear their cruel laughs which aroused anger in my heart. I felt as if they were mocking at us, telling us that we are powerless. I unsheathed my sword and jumped off the branch in anger and fell to the ground with a thud. I shrieked in pain. I knew that I had sprained my ankle.

"Why did you jump off, Alex?" Jack asked in a strained voice.

"I didn't answer as I did not have the energy to do so. Silence succeeded Jack's question. My sword lay next to me.

"Alex do you hear me…Are you OKAY?"

One by one my friends climbed down the tree.

Jason…fire… quick." Roalf said worriedly.

"But…"

"The giants are far away, there's no danger. Now fire please," Jack said.

My eyes were closed trying to bear the pain. I didn't have the energy to get up. I took the sword in my hand and held it tightly and tried to seek its energy. It worked. I got the energy to get up. Even that slight movement made me yelp.

I pictured my friends beside me. I saw Jack taking out water from his bag and Jason bringing out a couple of medicines from his bag. Roalf was attending to my ankle. He twisted it a bit to check the damage. I screamed instantly.

"Not helping."

I tried to move my foot voluntarily but in vain. I could not sense it, it had become numb.

"Why did you jump, Alex?" Jason asked.

"I jumped in anger. I'm going to seek revenge. They were going to tear us to pieces, but this will happen the other way round now. How dare they dream to kill the Lords who maintain the equilibrium of this world? I will kill the Giants with the holy sword of Iregor," I shouted in anger. With that last shout I had drained off my energy. Murmuring something I lied down on the wet ground and fell unconscious.

My dream went like this: *The Moon was high in the sky, glistening like a gem. The swiftly moving breeze brushed my hair. Nature's holy gifts talked to their brother wind via their sanctified methods. Oak and Elm trees on either side of me flapped their iridescent wings like beautiful birds. The sand under my feet rose in the air due to the breeze which set up a convection current. The dry leaves fallen on the ground however were not swept by the current; these just made a ruffling noise, for a reason. They crumpled under my feet as I ran deep into a dark forest, tired and panting and armed with nothing except my clothes and armor.*

Well, why wouldn't I run? A fifteen feet huge monster with a fat belly was chasing me. He had two feet on each leg, egg shaped eyes with no eye balls, huge forward ears and three horns on his head. His skin was twisted and scaled all over and his body was glowing with a faint tinge of green and yellow. A faint smell of garlic was filled in the air.

The monster held a scepter in his right hand which had a large unblemished ruby fixed into it. I nick-named him Philips. Ha! How I remembered Mrs. Philips. She was my bullying ex-Science and Math teacher who always was confused about the long homework she gave us for writing. When she used to correct the answer sheets of our homework, she would undoubtedly ask – was this the homework I gave you?" I would think no more of the matter as it was my every day's work to bear the banter.

She always boasted about herself and what not! I thought Mrs. Philips to be a person who knew nothing about the world but herself. The story of the Battle of the Sumter Fort was not unknown in the Fymland Valley. I often used to joke with my friends about Mrs. Philips being suited for the post of modern Maut (The King of Ganohan). But the only difference was that she lacked a huge giant like body.

I saw a sword dug deep into the ground nearby a tree but something was inscribed on it. After a moment I realized that it was my weapon – The Holy Sword of Iregor. I could also see what was written on it- Oh! God... The two words – "by Roalf" were shabbily written in blood! Roalf, my favorite teacher at school, the one who

I knew at school as Mr. Thomas, the one who turned out to be the Lord of wind... Anyways let's continue with the story as Monster Philips is getting closer. I was too astonished that I couldn't even get myself moving properly. But I knew I had to continue or die in a painful way. For sure I didn't want to take my last breath in the hands of an obese monster.

I moved toward the sword to defend myself from Philips. But before I could reach it I tripped over a rock and fell to the ground with a thud. I shrieked in pain, "Aahh!" I was just inches away from my sword. If I could just get hold of it, I would gain all my energy back and be an equal rival for my opponent. But the problem was that I didn't know how to fight. I desperately tried to reach its hilt but I couldn't. Philips was advancing towards me. I tried once again but in vain. The inscription on the sword's blade was much clearer to be seen. I realized that it was written in blood. But besides the inscription there was something else. But, I had no time to know what it was.

I felt a shadow on my back and turned. The moon was blocked from my view when Philips jumped high in the air, with his scepter right above my heart. And then down went the scepter deep into my heart. My vision blurred. The last thing that I heard was the monster's distant laughter.

I got up perspiring profusely. I could still hear that monster's wicked laughter. I was panting. I looked around and saw Jack and Jason sitting on a big rock discussing something. I tried to get up. My ankle flared in pain and I remembered that I had sprained my ankle jumping off a branch from the tree which was at least twenty feet high. Jack and Jason rushed to me saying, "Oh! Careful, you're hurt."

With their help I got up and sat on a rock. I stretched my legs and saw that my foot was wrapped in an elastic bandage. The pain was much less than it was the previous night.

We were still in the forest which was now comparatively brighter. Some sunrays could now reach the ground. I looked up. The canopy was not so thick. I looked at Jack and Jason again. Realizing the absence of Roalf I asked, "Where's Roalf?"

Jason answered, "He's gone to check out the forest. He thinks that we are quite near the end of it."

"He worked quite a lot to heal your ankle. He rubbed some herbs on your ankle and bandaged it. It's good that we carried some basic medical supplies with us," Jack said.

"He gave you some elixir. A good potion – He had said…Yeah, I know, Magic." Jason said drily.

Just then I saw Roalf coming out from between two big trees ahead us. He looked full of energy. I could see a smile on his bright face. His clothes were dirty with stains of mud, so was mine.

"How's your ankle?" he asked.

"It's better now," I answered.

"So are you ready to move? We are quite near the end of the forest and our surroundings are safe."

"But he's not ready," Jack and Jason complained.

I interrupted saying, "I'm ready. I want to reach Iregor as soon as possible."

"Your ankle would get healed completely there," Roalf said.

Jack and Jason helped me get up. I had some difficulty in walking but I eventually got over it. I was limping on my foot. The previous night's incident had infused hatred for the Giants in my heart. Their conversation had really made me angry. I wanted to kill them then and there. But I wasn't prepared yet. I didn't even know how to swing my sword which I hoped I would learn soon in Iregor. I was pretty excited to see Iregor because it was where my sword was forged.

But I was pretty shaken by my nightmare. It was unusual. The monster…the forest…my sword…these were all the same as what we have seen in reality. Glore had told me that we lived in a world where dreams could come true but I didn't want this dream to come true. I did not mention anything about this dream to my friends because they would get worried for me and I had already given them enough trouble.

I was brought back to reality from my own thoughts when Roalf said, "I was pretty taken aback by what you said last night before getting unconscious. You have really become hard, Alex, like your father. I had seen Sior and Leon in Jack and Jason, but you've progressed very well. I miss my old friends. We were a nemesis to the giants."

I had nothing to say and so was silent.

"And now when we get to Iregor you all will receive training in your own fields. I hope they welcome us. But initially they wouldn't recognize us."

"By the way Roalf, why do those giants glow in the night?" I asked.

"That is due to the high phosphorus content in their body. Giants live only on animals and humans; the only perfect carnivores. Phosphorus formed a major constituent of their excretory waste material. Naturally phosphorus is excreted by them in large quantities through their skin when they exert themselves and phosphorus catches fire in the presence of oxygen." Roalf replied.

After a while we saw the beginning of a new landscape. I was happy to come out of that gloomy forest. We could see the bright Sun after many days. My face was shining with brilliance. My ankle did not bother me now. It had partially healed and I seemed to have developed a resistance to pain.

We had come to a cliff, below which was situated the beautiful valley of Iregor.

CHAPTER 14

Iregor

"You see there", he said pointing downwards, "that's the valley of Iregor."

But Roalf didn't know that we had already recognized it. I could feel the excitement in his voice. His face was glowing under the bright Sun. His eyes were sparkling. The little benevolent gentleman was almost quivering with happiness. But this man, one would say, could never play a noticeable part, or rise to fame in any sphere. And yet, in reaching such a conclusion, one would have been terribly wrong. For this man, straightforward and inconspicuous as he seemed, would play a major part in the destiny of this world.

"It hasn't changed a bit. I remember it exactly. This is the place where I was born. And you see there," he said pointing at an angle to the sky, "Those are the Egor Mountains. That is where the ruby and Alex's sword was forged. Let's go down. I hope they recognize me." But my eyes caught something which made me leap with joy; I saw a water body – A river. The river cut through the valley and its tributaries divided the valley into six parts. Excited I asked Roalf, "which river is that?"

"You would be shocked if I tell you. That's River Egil but here it's called Egorian River because Egor Mountains are where it originates."

"Really!" I, Jason and Jack exclaimed in unison.

"Yeah, it seeps underground in the Bulkite Forests and then it rises to land again in the Egilium Forests." I was certainly shocked. I marveled at nature. A river that runs underground – I had never heard about something like that.

It took us a little time to get down the cliff as it was very steep. Luckily Jason had a rope in his bag. He tied it to a boulder and then Roalf started his descent. I didn't understand why Roalf used a rope to get down. He could have easily flown down. Jason was the next to go. He used his walking stick to get down quickly. Jason was followed by me.

My eyes were fixed on the Egor Mountains. They looked like a mass of huge irregular grey triangles curved at the edges. Their peaks were snow-covered and were hidden by the clouds. The mountains had a dark patch on them which looked like the shadow of something huge. From the mountains there originated seven waterfalls of which one of them was, I guessed, the Egorian River (Egil River). I would say that these mountains were a perfect place for an extraordinary ruby to be forged.

Just then I lost my grip on the rope and was about to fall when Jack caught me by my shoulder.

"Careful Alex, You're already hurt. Don't give your body more pain." Jack said that with such love and affection for me that I could not help but feel guilty for not being careful.

I shifted my eyes from the mountains towards the ground. Roalf had already touched the bottom and Jason was about to do so. I hurried and reached the base in no time. The very next second Jack was with us.

We faced huge black solid gates that blocked entrance into Iregor. The corners of the gates had a projection upwards to which was attached a board that said, "Welcome to Iregor". The extra thick tall walls that held the solid gates bounded entire Iregor.

We moved towards the gates and just as we were going to try to open them, there appeared a rusty lock on the gates out of nowhere. Roalf looked surprised and within no time there appeared a smile on his face.

"Iregor hasn't changed a bit."

"So do you know how to open this door?" Jason asked.

"Of course, I know. I have spent about thirty years in Iregor and I wouldn't know its secrets?"

"Please open it then," I said quickly.

"Okay. But first you should promise me that you would keep this secret to yourselves because Iregor allows no strangers to enter it."

"Okay, we promise," Jack answered for all of us. Convinced, Roalf moved forward and tapped on the lock in a musical sequence. Immediately the gates were unlocked and moved outwards revealing a road inside.

For about a hundred yards there was nothing to get excited about. On either side of the road there extended a field of smooth, rich green tall grasses. Not a single life form could be seen. It was lonely. The road was marked by pebbles. I was quite happy to be in Iregor. But what would be in store here, I didn't know. Roalf would certainly lead us there. Presently, the people of Iregor would certainly ask questions, but will we be able to answer them? We might even have to reveal our identity.

And then we saw 'the inhabited' Iregor. Gradually, small houses built upon tiny mounds and hillocks came into sight. These extended on either side of the road. As we passed them we could see that a series of steps led to the doorway of a house. The layout of each house was almost the same, something completely different from that in Fymland.

"Yes, Iregor is completely different from Fymland." Roalf said as if reading my thoughts.

"So when you came to Fymland did you find it strange?" I asked enquiringly.

"Not really," Roalf said, "I had been to Fymland a number of times, and after all it was Dane's home you see. It was easy for me to adapt."

"Oh", I said.

The forlorn tract was slowly fading away. A young man with thick eyebrows and brown hair was approaching us on a bicycle. He nodded his head as he passed us. There was a smile on his face but he looked at us strangely. He was the first man I had seen in Iregor. We nodded.

Roalf asked him loudly, "It would be very kind of you if you told us what time it is."

"The young man stopped on his bicycle and said looking at this watch, "Well, it is…. half past three."

"Could you tell us the route to the market?" Roalf asked.

"Yes, yes why not. Take this road it will lead you to the river. Use the bridge and get to the other end. Take the first right, then the left and there you are, in the market."

"Thank you."

"Just entered Iregor?" The man asked.

"Ye…ah." Roalf said stammering.

"Good afternoon," the young man said and cycled on.

We started to move again and Roalf was much more confident. I looked at Jack. He was always confident, except for the time when we were in The Bulkite Forests. As for Jason, he was always carefree. I always felt euphoric when I was in the company of my friends. We all cared for each other.

Just as advised by the man on the bicycle, the road led us to the river. My spirits rose. All I wanted to do was to just dive into this river. The river was quite wide and deep but I felt that it was inviting me to make contact.

"So where's the bridge?" Jason spoke after a long while.

"There." Jack said pointing towards the right. The bridge that we saw was at the end of another road. "Let's go there then." Roalf said.

"I prefer the river." I said which made everybody smile.

"Oh yes Alex, why not." Jack said.

"I say, we shall race to the other end of the river, Alex by river, Roalf by wind, Jack and me by the bridge. What do you say?" Jason said smiling.

"I wouldn't fly because I would be easily noticed," Roalf said.

"Okay Roalf, but I bet that I'm going to be the first to reach across." I said confidently.

"We'll see that." Roalf said challengingly.

"First we shall get to the bridge." Jack said.

They started walking leaving me beside a house at the bank of a river. When they reached, the whole party said together, "Get, Set, Go."

I dived into the river and felt the first touch of water after what seemed to be a long time. I was vigorously stroking my hands and legs. Every now and then I would go underwater. I found no difficulty in breathing underwater as the back of my ears worked like gills of a fish. I looked towards the bridge. I saw Jack taking the lead. He was an equal challenge for me.

A short distance to the shore was left. I gave a final push to my body and swam with such might that I flipped out of water and landed on dry grass at a distance. I turned back and saw Jack touch the grass. I was the first. I had won the challenge. "I'm the first." I yelled.

My friends came running towards me. "You're quite fast in water, Alex." Jack said patting me on the shoulder.

"Thanks." I said.

"Alex, but why aren't you wet?" Jason asked with surprise.

"What a miracle!" Jack exclaimed. "Or is it magic?"

"Well –" Just as I was going to say Roalf interrupted me.

"It's not a miracle. It's his power. He doesn't get wet as his skin can absorb significant amounts of moisture and he can very well breathe underwater like a fish."

"That's great." Jack said.

"Yeah, you've got awesome powers, man!" Jason said.

"Yeah, but I can't barbecue like you, with bare hands."

We all started laughing heartily.

"I'm thirsty and we have run out of our supplies." Jack said resting on his knees.

"Don't worry; you can drink the river water." I said.

"Is it clean?" He asked.

"It's very clean. No harm could come from it."

Jack filled water in the bottles and drank some.

"Now let's go to the market," Roalf said.

"But what are we going to do after reaching there?" Jason asked.

"We'll see." Roalf said and started to move. We followed him. The houses on the other side of the river were the same except that they were bigger. I could spot some people. Some were jogging; some were watering the plants outside their small houses. They looked quite different. Men kept long hair, something which was forbidden in the Flareds. They wore loose gown like clothes that were of much older fashion. As we passed them they looked at us as if they had never seen people like us before. Well that was true. Or did they look at us because of our clothes? Our clothes were dirty, yes, with stains of mud. I had spoiled my best outfit after all.

"I haven't seen any cars in Iregor until now." Jason started up a conversation.

"And you will never see one." Roalf said laughing.

"Why?" Jason asked astonished.

"Iregor is not like Fymland. It does not use any modern machinery. It still uses horses and horse drawn carts for transport. Iregor has now started to use bicycles as we have seen one earlier. Apart from that I don't think they would welcome any other form of mechanized transport. You've entered a different world, my boys. A much older world. A world where the first swords were forged and the first lords were born. Iregor is proud of its history. It will change with time, that's for sure, but at the speed of a tortoise."

"But why?" Jack asked.

"Why?" Roalf laughed and then continued, "Isn't it better. There is no pollution in Iregor. Traditions are still followed. Even their clothing is different. In

Fymland guns are used but here only swords, spears and other weaponry forged by Blacksmiths. It may be weird to you but get used to it, because this is how warriors live." We kept quiet and walked. Roalf was actually right in what he said. Living in a pollution free natural environment was so good.

After following the instructions of the man who told us the way to the market, we finally reached it. Shops extended on either side of the road. The road was wider here. It was like a ramp that first sloped upwards and then sloped downwards to the ground. But I could see none of the shopkeepers in their shops. This was strange. Cattle were feeding on the fresh fruits and vegetables.

As we strolled down the slope we could see a great mass of people. All the shopkeepers must have assembled here – I guessed. We hurried toward them. As we closed up we realized that quite a lot of people had gathered there. We moved through the crowd and got to the front.

A stage was placed in the middle. It was covered with a pristine white cloth. Iregorians are very clean – I thought. The crowd opposite us, at the other end of the stage, comprised of people holding bouquets in their hands. I wondered what was going on there.

A sound of a trumpet startled me. A man somewhere from the crowd shouted saying, "Attention! Here comes the King of Iregor." Silence filled the air. Then clarinets and trumpets ended the silence. Nothing but music prevailed in the air. And then it suddenly stopped as a tall and fair man with long black hair that had beads at its ends, climbed the stage. He wore a royal dress. He had a muscular and lithe body. With big grey eyes he certainly looked a king.

As he stepped on to the stage he raised his hands and the huge crowd instantly started uttering praises. People threw bouquets at their king's feet. Then the king gestured with his right hand signaling them to stop.

"People of Iregor," He spoke for the first time and his voice was deep, effective and commanding. He's certainly a king – I thought once again.

He continued, "I've ruled for fifty years now and I've kept you all, my brave people, happy." He paused for a second and then continued, "Never for a second have I been laid back. Iregor is my soul. I've done everything to safeguard Iregor, have I not?"

"Yes you have!" The crowd yelled back. The king lacked complete elision. He spoke with a brilliant eloquence. That was affecting the people. His voice was like magic; a bungalow in the middle of an oasis – I harked back to Glore's words. But it was certainly not ethereal. His speech was perpetual and eternal.

"And I do the same now," He continued, "As the Giants call for war I answer it! Iregor answers it! But we do not attack. We stay and defend Iregor like we always have. As always, we shall win! We shall win!" The crowd launched into praises again; some were shouting, "We shall win, yes we shall!"

The king raised his hand and signaled them to stop. Just then the Lord of Wind beside me murmured, "Theromir."

The king turned towards us and asked, "Did someone call me?"

Jason pinched his right ear and Jack cursed under his breath. The crowd became silent. The king once again asked, "Who called my name?"

"I did," The Lord of the Wind climbed up the stage and came face to face with the king. "Yes, I did, Theromir. Don't you remember me, my brother?"

"I don't know who you are; get off the stage young man." The king said in a deep commanding voice. I could feel that he felt insulted.

"I'm your brother, Theromir."

"I have no brother and the one that I had had died long ago." Theromir said coldly.

"No! He hasn't died. If you don't remember who I am, then I hope you remember this." Saying that Roalf extended his hand as if holding a weapon and in his fist materialized a bow on which were embedded many symbols and on his back a quiver of arrows could be seen. The bow was very big, almost of Roalf's size. It had the shine of pure gold. The symbols on it were glowing under the bright Sun. The quiver on Roalf's back was filled with arrows; may be a hundred arrows, I guessed. Maybe it would never get empty. Only the shaft of the arrows could be seen. The arrowheads, I knew were deadly.

"Roalf." The king murmured. The entire crowd gave a gasp and murmured, "Roalf".

Then the king's face reddened with anger. He burst out. "Why have you come now? You had abandoned our homeland long ago. You had fled to Fymland which was always different from Iregor. Go back and stay there. You're not welcome here."

Roalf, filled with anger, said, "Brother, I never abandoned my home land. I was there in Fymland because of my oath to my beloved friend Dane. And Iregor would not have been like this, preparing for battle with the cursed giants every year, if you had sent for help to Fymland during the battle of Sumter Fort. But I don't hold a grudge against you for that. I have not come here to seek the throne. I have come here to destroy the ruby of Ganohan." He paused and then holding Theromir by his shoulder he continued, "This has to end now brother, we cannot just defend Iregor all the time; we have to attack. Send word to Maut that we need time to prepare ourselves and that we wish to battle in two years from now."

"But we just can't do this with a small army of men and one Lord. Your friends had died fifty years ago." Theromir said.

"Who said that I'm the only Lord? Alex…Jason… Jack, Roalf said looking at us."

We climbed up the stage and Roalf introduced us to Theromir and the crowd. "This is Jack, son of Sior, the Lord of Earth and the wielder of the Giant Slayer."

Jack instantly bowed and held out both of his hands in which his axe materialized, "Jack at your service."

"This is Jason, son of Leon, the Lord of Fire and the wielder of the Fire Knight." Jason too bowed and held his walking stick perpendicular to the stage which changed into a spear, "Jason at your service."

"And this is Alex, son of Dane, the Lord of Water and the wielder of…its better you show them yourself Alex."

I took out the Holy Sword from its sheath in a swift move and raised it above my shoulder. It was shining with that watery blue tinge that was stunning to look at and gave it a hallowed feel. The sword felt quite heavy in my hands but I could hold it. Silence fell over the crowd and I said, "Alex at your service."

Roalf was bearing a big smile on his face and he asked the King of Iregor, "Are you convinced, my brother?"

The king answered slowly, "Yes I am, Roalf."

Theromir remained quiet, so did the entire crowd. They were pretty astonished. But I knew that they were dancing with joy inside their hearts. Roalf looked at us and nodded. We were partially successful in our quest.

"So do we receive shelter?" Roalf asked.

CHAPTER 15

I Receive Training from Glore

Two months had passed since we entered Iregor. Lord Theromir was taking good care of us. Word was sent through a royal messenger to the Giants that Iregor would be ready for war with them in two years' time. On his return the messenger had informed Lord Theromir that King Maut had agreed to the treaty with an amusing look on his face. Since then there has been no further discussion on Giants and the upcoming war. We were being well fed and apart from watching the soldiers practice every day we had no specific assignments to work on.

Roalf decided that we should build a house near the Igor River and not stay at the Castle as it will keep us busy for a few days and help us develop skills in building work. We built a small house borrowing the materials from our Iregorian neighbors. It was cozy and warm inside and was just enough for the four of us.

Our routine had not changed even a bit. We had been to the Royal Palace of Iregor several times to dine with the king and his family. The king had a son named Clarus. He had become a good friend of mine. As a young boy he had been quite exposed to war at an early age. I told him the tales of our adventure and he told me the various battles that the Iregorians had to fight against the giants.

It was below freezing point now. The road was covered with snow. It was ten in the morning and the sky was covered with dense clouds. Winter had begun in Iregor. I wore a winter jacket made by the Iregorians which was very different from the stuff available in Fymland. They were made of gossamer. I wore black trousers that were my favorite and black gloves on my hands. In addition to this, Roalf asked me to wrap my neck with a scarf to protect myself from cold.

"It's very difficult to bear Iregorian winter. It's not like Fymland," he said. And I found him right; it was biting cold that made it difficult to venture outside. But I needed some fresh air and so decided to take a stroll. The Iregorian Mountains were now completely covered with snow. My ankle had completely healed since I started receiving Iregorian treatment. There was not a soul around me. The river that I was so happy about had frozen. But it did not disappoint me because a touch from my Sword was all that was needed to turn ice into water. It was the energy of the Sword that made it happen. I wanted to touch and feel the water over my body. I bent extending my left hand to touch water. But before I could touch the water it spouted on to my palm and coursed down. The water felt very cold to touch. I decided against taking a dip. I closed my left palm and the spout vanished. The river turned back to ice the moment I withdrew the Sword from water. The same transformation would have happened if I had plunged my Sword into snow and withdrawn it. My powers were growing as I was becoming conscious of their residence in me.

My Iregorian home was completely covered with snow. I entered it. My body regained its warmth. I saw my friends sitting by the fireplace. I took off my Jacket and scarf and hung them on a wooden stand and sat beside my friends.

"Hey." I said.

"How was your walk?" Jack asked as he held out his hands close to the fire.

"It was good. But it's a snow world outside. There was not a soul on the road and the river is frozen. Pretty bad winter."

Roalf said laughing, "There's no bad winter; it's only different weather effected by nature."

"Roalf, I have a question…If Lord Theromir is your brother then why doesn't he have the powers which you have. After all you both are the children of the previous Lord of the wind."

"Good question," he said filling his cup with warm tea. "Most of the powers of my father were imparted to me. It was my father's choice. But who said that Theromir doesn't have powers. He is a well-trained warrior and a top class magician. He is as strong as I am."

"A magician?" Jack questioned.

"Yes. All of them are trained to become magicians but Theromir was born a magician. Actually, greater than a magician. He is someone else." I was quite interested in Lord Theromir. We were lost in thoughts when Jason came in between.

"This thing still confuses me," Jason said thoughtfully, "If Ronkar and Batchels had taken the road in the forest then why didn't we meet them in Iregor."

"Because they must have taken a diversion," Jack said as if it was as simple as that.

"But that was the only road," Jason said.

"They are Giants Jason, they don't care about nature. They must have trampled some trees and made their way to Ganohan", Roalf replied.

"Even if they had taken the road to Iregor, they could not have entered it because they don't know the secret," I replied. Our conversation was cut off by the knock on the door.

"I'll check," I said. I got up and went up to the door and opened it. I saw the face of the magician and scientist who had given me the holy sword of Iregor.

"It's Glore!" I exclaimed happily, "Come on in Glore."

He followed me to the fireplace and Roalf eagerly hugged him. "I knew you would come," Roalf said smiling.

"I knew that you would find your way to Iregor. Any difficulties?" Glore asked.

"Nothing to complain about," Jack said.

"How did you come here?" Jason asked.

"Through a portal."

"The portal dropped you directly inside?" I asked.

"No. It dropped me at the gates and then I went to the palace and got to know where you were. By the way, the king is quite fascinated with you all." Glore replied. Glore knew the secret codes to the gates of Iregor. Why wouldn't he know, he travels round the world.

"Come sit down," Roalf said offering a seat next to the fire.

"Where's the golden sphere that I gave you?" The magician asked.

"It's with me." I said but I did not show it to Glore, "It hasn't been of any use to us until now."

"Trust me; it's going to be very helpful to you all."

"Hope so," I murmured.

"Are you the only magician?" Jack asked.

"No. There are many like me. In fact, there are two in Iregor itself. They are going to help me train you all." Glore said.

"Oh!"

"How far is Ganohan from here, Glore?" Jason asked tapping his walking stick continually on the floor.

"About thirty miles. Iregor is the closest place to Ganohan," Glore replied sliding his hands over his long white beard.

"How many inhabited places exist around this part of the world?" I asked.

"There are many. To the north of Iregor you have Ganohan. To the west, there is Garyland, the birth place of your father, Jack. To the east, there is Ferogor, the place where Jason's father was born. To the south you have Fymland, the land of Alex's father. Beyond that, there are many."

"Have you seen the Giants of late? Are they as strong as before?" Roalf asked.

"Yes, I had done some sneaking in Ganohan before coming to Iregor. They are quite a lot and their power is the same as before. These kids have to get trained to face them effectively," he said worriedly.

"So what are we waiting for?" I said as I got up, "Let's train now, my friends." Jason, Jack and I held our hands together and said, "We are ready."

"Let's go to the palace then because the palace has the training rooms." Glore said.

He took us straight to the corridor in the palace where the rooms were located. He did not even allow us to spend a minute looking at the statues and chandeliers in the palace. I had seen them earlier but they still fascinated me.

The first room we came to had a door which prevented us from looking inside. "That's for you Jack. Get inside. You'll find your teacher there, a magician just like me. His name is Romeg."

"Good luck." We wished him and moved on. The next room was just like the previous one from outside.

"That's for you Jason, your teacher's name is Gondlier, a magician again."

"The best to you." I wished him. The next one was for Roalf as he went inside on his own. When we started moving again, I asked, "Would Roalf need a teacher."

"Why would he? He is a well-trained archer."

That was sensible. Glore was the teacher for me. We came to a room and I opened it and entered. What I saw was a wide room with nothing in it and bounded by three walls; the other end I couldn't see. There were no windows and yet the room was bright.

"Let's start. It's eleven now, we have time till one o' clock."

"Okay."

He asked me to jog as long as I could toward the unbounded end of the room. It was like running through a portal that never left this room. I came to a stop after a while being tired but Glore pushed me saying, "Come on! Keep going." I wanted to say, "Do you want me to drop dead?" But I kept my mouth shut as he was the magician and the teacher.

After a long while Glore asked me to stop. "You can rest now." I was completely worn-out; beads of sweat poured down my cheeks, my mouth was open and I was panting. I sat down on the cold ground and drank some water. I felt re-energized. I regained my energy whenever I drank water. That was one of the powers I had. But I had got still more to discover about my strengths.

I got up and went to Glore. "We practice with the sword now, so draw it out," he said. Following his instructions I unsheathed my sword. As soon as it was out of the sheath, it felt heavy in my hands.

Glore said, "Now practice arching your sword from ground to shoulder a hundred times using both your hands." I was completely baffled by what he said. Surely I was not going to take part in any weight lifting competition nor was I interested in developing a muscular body. Reading my irritated expression Glore said, "Listen to what I say. It would be better that way."

I did what he asked me to do. Glore then said, "Now hold the sword steadily with one hand for as long as possible close to the ground but without touching its tip to the ground." But that was too difficult and I let the sword touch ground within no time. I changed hands and the same thing happened.

Finally Glore signaled me to stop and said, "That's enough for today, go home and we meet tomorrow here at the same time. And don't mention anything about our practice to your friends."

My hands were paining. "A question," I said.

"Yes?"

"What's that symbol on that sphere on your staff?"

"The symbol is of two stars bound together meaning, allegiance to truth and nature."

"Thanks."

I left the room and found my friends in the corridor. Jason and Jack were wet with sweat but Roalf was quite fresh. I sighed.

"How was it?" I asked.

"Pretty bad." Jason replied.

"Yeah, pretty bad for me too." Jack replied. We spoke no more and went straight to our house on foot.

The next day, I felt Glore had advanced on his teachings. The starters were the same; warm ups but the jog time was increased and it felt like an eternity. The next thing was to drink water and regain energy. After that as Glore saw that I could lift my sword very well in my hands he taught me how to hold it. That was quite simple - Hold the sword by its grip.

"Keep your weapon in front of you. You will want your body twisted sideways, with your weapon towards your opponent. This makes your body a smaller target and also gives you a better range with your weapon. There is no reason to have your unarmed side facing your opponent, it only invites a hit." Glore advised me.

I practiced as he said. I was good with this technique. Subsequent techniques were difficult. Glore taught me how to attack and the various combos. He showed a demo of them with his staff which he transformed into a sword. All the magic that Glore used to perform frightened me earlier, but now I was getting used to it. I was transforming into my true self. Brave and powerful, just like my father.

I practiced all the techniques of which Glore showed a demo one by one. Glore had a problem with me on each one of them; he spotted mistakes in postures, speed, force and the like. It was getting too demanding, but I knew that I would eventually achieve it.

Six months passed and I was greatly improving. I had begun to like the training. Glore was happy about it. At times, during my training Glore would make statues of miniature Giants and tell me to implement all that I had learnt. But when I performed some combo blows on the statues, not even a scar would appear.

"You excel in all your techniques but you lack power. Exert greater force on your blows," Glore would counsel me. After days of practice, I could finally cut across the statues. My conversation with Jack, Jason and Roalf was limited. One of the reasons was that we didn't have enough time to talk to each other. The second reason was that all of us have been ordered by our respective teachers to discuss nothing about the training. Roalf had no teacher but still he didn't talk much with us. As for Clarus, I would meet him a couple of times in the palace but we couldn't start up a conversation as I was always in a hurry.

The cold winter slowly changed into a warm and beautiful spring. One day, during my training I had to fight Glore for which I wasn't prepared at all. "Today you'll fight me. We'll see how much you have learnt. Don't disappoint me."

I was shocked. How could I fight my own teacher who was a magician? He would obviously be more powerful than me. "Are you crazy Glore? How can I fight you?" I asked.

"The greatest drawback of a fighter is lack of confidence. If you have confidence in yourself, then you can fight even the most powerful person in this world. Now take your position. Don't disappoint me."

"But what if I hurt you accidentally?"

"That's not going to happen. There's no need for you to worry."

"Okay." I drew my sword and it did not feel heavy as I was now used to handling it every day. It was now part of me. I increased the distance between my legs a little and then held the sword pointing its apex towards my opponent. Glore was the first to attack. He slapped the side of my waist with his staff which made me fall. It was already beginning to pain. "I wasn't ready." I gave an excuse. "Get up!" Glore shouted. I instantly got up and again Glore attacked. This time I blocked the blow but still it made me stumble, his blow was so powerful. Glore kept on attacking and I kept on blocking. A sort of rally was going on. Finally bored by the rally, I jumped high in the air and brought my sword down in a swift move. But Glore blocked it and then pushed me down. I fell hard on my back.

"That was good. Remember you can't win a battle if you don't attack." Glore said, "Come on get up."

This time I attacked first and Glore blocked it. But I didn't stop. I kept on performing the combos that Glore had taught me. Then suddenly Glore moved his staff towards me but I side-stepped and spotted Glore's open waist. That was an easy target. I moved my sword horizontally towards Glore's waist. But it was blocked by an invisible barrier. So that was the secret of Glore for not being injured. We both stopped and Glore said with a mocking smile, "Now this would be something new for you." He instantly disappeared. Shocked, I turned around to look for him.

Just then I felt a force on my back which made me fall. I recognized the force – it was of Glore's staff. So this was his trick. He must have attacked from somewhere behind me. I got up and turned. This time I was attacked from the opposite direction. I got up and turned again. Now the force came from my left. I got up angrily and then again I was knocked down by the force coming from my right. "Where are you Glore?" I shouted, "Show yourself. Don't fight like a coward!" This time the force came from behind me. I was pretty angry at him.

Then something struck me. Glore was following an attacking pattern which was first from North, then South, then West and then from East. If this time he had attacked from North then the next would be from South. It was predictable. I tightened my grip over the sword. I got up facing North. I felt a slight commotion behind me. In that fraction of second I turned and moved my sword straight in the air. It was blocked and that was due to the invisible protective barrier of Glore. He materialized before me with a smiling face.

I asked, "How was it?"

He answered, "Very good. This is how Maut fights in the battle. It is his deadliest technique. This would be very helpful to you. But you're yet to master the most important thing."

CHAPTER 16

I Fight My Lord Friends

"And what's that?" I asked, thinking. I had learnt everything that Glore had taught me. Then what was the thing that was still left for me to learn?

"Do you know how to use your powers?" Glore asked me.

"I know three of them. First - I can swim although I have never learnt swimming. Second - I can breathe underwater. Third - I get energy from water and it obeys my command. That's all I know."

"That's pretty less you know. These are of no use in war."

"Will you teach me how to use the other powers?"

"No. I cannot teach you. They are your powers and not mine," he answered.

"But how can you be sure that I have more powers?" I asked plainly.

"Because you're the Lord of Water. Breathing underwater and not getting wet can be possible even by my magic. That's nothing unusual. There is something else that makes you the Lord of Water, something which no one in this world can do. Discover it on your own."

"Hope time will tell."

"Remember one thing - You have boundless powers. You have to discover them yourself. By the way there's a pool for you and I give you an hour with it. Use it your way." I turned back as he said and saw a medium-sized asymmetrical pool with glistening blue water in it.

"Wish you luck," saying that he left the room leaving me alone. I decided to get into the pool and relax. As there was no need for me to undress I jumped into the pool at once. I swam for a little while. My muscles relaxed and the pain that I had in my back was on the wane.

I went underwater, no problem in breathing. I couldn't find out the reason for it being possible. I saw the base of the pool. I swam downwards and sat down at the base so that I could think cut off from the noise of the normal world. I didn't feel any upward force. I was completely free in water.

I closed my eyes and thought. What was it that was so special about me? What was it that made me the Lord of Water? I always loved to be in water. My bathroom in the Flareds would always be carpeted with water. Jack and Jason wanted it to be dry. They would often tell me that I was being very unhygienic. But I couldn't help it.

In spite of the absence of my friends I never felt alone. Even now at the bottom of the pool I didn't feel alone; it was certainly due to water. But when there was no water near me? I kept thinking…and then it struck me. As Roalf had said that the Egorian River seeps underground and then rises again to land in Egilium Forests. And during rainfall, some of the water must have seeped underground and remained there. So that is the reason why I never felt alone; water was part of me.

I remembered Glore's words, "You don't need a river or a sea to use your powers." He had said that during the start of our adventure. He was right. I didn't need a sea or a river to use my powers, all I needed was water and that was everywhere.

Even this time, Glore was right. I realized that my powers were boundless. Even if I had not discovered them, yet I had discovered the main reason for me being the Lord of Water. And that itself means that even if I had not commanded my powers, I would still know of their existence. Yes, my powers were rising in me.

I had realized long ago who I was. My blood flowed with confidence at this thought. I imagined that my eyes were blazing with a blue flame. I removed my sword from its sheath. Its sparkling ruby could be very well seen underwater. The blue hue camouflaged with the pool water.

The Holy Sword of Iregor was not used during the battles between the Giants and the previous lords. No one knew about its existence. My connection with the Holy Sword of Iregor was natural. I was quite confident that it was not possible for it to stay away from me.

Maybe this sword was made for me. Maybe it was destined to come into my hands.

I closed my eyes doing nothing. I just wanted the feel of water.

After a long pause, I opened my eyes. An hour had passed. And my time with the pool was over too. I got up and allowed the water to push me out. I jumped out of the pool. And again I wasn't wet. I saw Glore open the door and come in.

"Your time's over." He said as he came close to me.

"I know. The time was too much for me."

"Why can I see a blue flame in your eyes?" He asked smiling slowly.

"If that is so, then it's very good." I answered confidently.

"So you've mastered all of them."

"I've practiced none of them but I somehow seem to have mastered all of them," I said smiling.

Glore gave me a smile that I had never seen. He came and hugged me. "Very good Alex, that was imminent. I'm proud of you. But use your powers wisely, or else they can also bring your downfall. Get me?

"Yeah" I said sheepishly.

"We have to go to another room now," he said hurriedly.

"But why?" I asked worried.

"Oh there's no need to worry. You'll know when we go to the other room."

Following Glore, I exited my training room and he closed the door behind me. We skipped the next room and entered the following room. As I entered the room, I saw Jack. He was different. He looked sturdier and taller. He looked matured. But his face was the same as always – A circular face that had white skin stretched over it, a small nose, brown eyes, thick eyebrows and fluffy cheeks. His face was glowing and his eyes were sparkling.

"Hey Jack! You look taller and sturdier," I said.

"You too," he replied. That meant that I had changed in my appearance. I hoped that I looked more handsome. Behind Jack I saw an old man who looked exactly like Glore except that he had his eyebrows joined. He had a staff with a brown sphere that had the same symbol as on Glore's green sphere. I guessed that he was Jack's teacher Romeg.

"So what are we here for?" I asked.

"Okay. Let's come to the point." Glore paused and then continued. "We have brought you together to test how much you've learnt."

"And how will you do that?" Jack asked.

"It's simple," Romeg spoke for the first time, his voice being very churlish. "We'll see you both fight."

"What!" Jack and I screamed. We both were shocked. It was hard for me to believe what Glore and Romeg were thinking. If I fight Jack then I would certainly have to fight Jason and Roalf too. But how can I fight my true and closest friends.

Then I slowly spoke, "But we would hurt each other in doing so. We both have real weapons."

"Don't worry about that. We have specially designed armors forged for both of you." Saying that he waved his hand and instantly a metal armor shining like gold automatically appeared on my body and a similar one on Jack's body.

"You've to get used to getting hurt. These small cuts should not matter because you're going to get a lot of them in the war. This is also helpful to both of you as the fight would make you aware of each other's weaknesses," Romeg said.

"Romeg is right. And I should tell you that in the room before this one Jason and Roalf are fighting each other." Glore said nodding his head. That was obvious.

"But where will we fight?" Jack asked.

"There." He pointed his fingers above my head that meant behind. I turned back and to my surprise instead of plane floor, a miniature playground having boulders with a miniature lake could be seen. Okay, now I understood. The main reason why Glore and Romeg wanted us to fight was to see how we would use our skills in the battle.

Sadly, I spoke to my friend, "I don't want to fight you Jack but ....."

"Don't worry Alex," Jack intervened, "This is going to help us. So let's do it with full energy." Jack said confidently. Looking at Jack, my confidence level rose and I was ready to fight.

I walked to the fighting place and took my position near the lake. Jack took his place at the far end of the playground. Glore stood in the middle and Jack and I came up to him. "Listen to the rules," he said, "First, attacking at the level of neck is not allowed. Second, you cannot remove your armor. Third, we give you ten minutes to fight and after that when we say "stop" you will stop. Do you two agree?"

"Yes," we said in unison.

He moved away from the playground, to stand beside Romeg. He then said, "Your time starts now."

Okay, I had to win anyhow. I took out my sword from its sheath in a swift move. I bent down and held my sword in front of me. I moved forward and so did Jack. And then suddenly I charged and performed an aerial attack on Jack. He blocked it and pushed me down, but I balanced myself. Jack instantly swung his giant axe at my waist. I jumped back and charged. This time I did a feint move to the left and then instantly swung my sword at the right. My sword clashed his armor, there was no harm done to him. So my blow was not so powerful.

I side-stepped to avoid the jab of The Giant Slayer, and then slashed Jack's right thigh. He did the same to me. My thigh flared with pain. I stumbled back and returned to my position by the lake and pointed my sword toward the water. Water ebbed out of the lake like a snake and covered my body in a slow swirling motion. It burnt as the water came in contact with open flesh on my thigh but then it healed itself showing newly developed skin. It wasn't a miracle, though.

I saw Jack standing away from me and watching the act in astonishment. And then he came to his senses within no time. I realized that although Jack was slow in his moves, he was accurate. Neither Jack nor I was going to win if we continued fighting like this. We had to use our powers. I waited for Jack to attack. He didn't move. After a while when I was frustrated standing and waiting, I charged; a blunder.

A wicked smile appeared on Jack's face. I stopped dead. Just then I felt something wrap my legs. I looked down. I was horrified. From the ground a twisting green stem with small green leaves was continuously wrapping my body. I tried to move but I couldn't. I struggled but it was of no use. It wrapped my whole body up to my chest. I felt my body being pricked by the thorns on the stem. My sword had fallen out of my hands. But that turned out to be good for me.

Nothing could separate me from my sword. As I gestured with my hand it moved toward me as if a suction pump was sucking it. I cut the creeper with a single blow. Jack was certainly amazed and so were the audience – Glore and Romeg. I smiled and returned to the lake. Then I advanced towards Jack. Every step I put on the ground, I felt water under my feet. But Jack didn't know that I was directing water from the lake towards him underground.

Jack charged but that was a mistake. I casually raised my left hand and to Jack's surprise, he was lifted in the air by water that burst from the ground. That was neither a geyser nor a hot spring but my power. I dropped him down. I made a mistake again by plummeting him to the ground because Jack is most powerful when he is on ground. I charged at him but I hit a wall. I felt as if my head was spinning. Exhausted I fell to the ground.

I heard Romeg say, "Very good. It's a tie. You both win." I got up rubbing my eyes. Glore came and hugged me saying, "Return to your room. You fight Jason in an hour." Following his instructions, I returned to my room. I didn't know where Jack was. On seeing that the pool was still there, I jumped into it and sat down at the base meditating.

After a while I met Jason in a different room, the one in which he had fought Roalf. He looked full of energy. He was with his teacher Gondlier and with Glore. Again Gondlier looked exactly like Glore except that his eyes were much bigger. His staff had an orange sphere with the same symbol of purity. For the battle between me and Jason the same ground was created with a lake. Again Glore explained us the rules and we took our positions, me near the lake and Jason at the far end.

We did the starters again. He bruised me, I bruised him. But Jason was not a person to wait. He instantly charged. This time I couldn't give him an underground water geyser because he was shifting his position every second as he ran towards me.

I dodged as he tried to pierce my armor with his spear. And then I hurled some of the water on his face by the gesture of my hand. He stepped back rubbing his face. He then pointed his spear at me. I could see its tip was turning red. And then suddenly a ball of fire was hurled at my body. I felt its power as it burned my body. I didn't yell. Glore and Gondlier as well as Jason were rushing towards me with a horrified face. I smiled and signaled them to stop.

The fire on my body extinguished.

"You cannot put a fire extinguisher on fire, Jason," said Glore.

He stopped dead. I charged at him with my sword raised. "Stop. Time's up" Glore shouted.

"It's a tie!" Jason's teacher exclaimed.

"Again?" I sighed.

"You nearly escaped death," Glore said tensed.

"Oh! Come on Glore," I laughed.

"It's not funny," Gondlier interrupted, "Jason's fire was a weak one. Had he made it stronger your powers would not have worked. He has deliberately made it weak."

I looked at Jason if he agreed; he didn't meet my eyes, which meant that what Gondlier said was true. Glore told me to return to my room and rest for an hour because next, I was going to fight Roalf whom I expected to be a formidable warrior.

I met Roalf in the room in which I fought Jack. And again the same playground for the brawl. Roalf had no teacher, so Glore was the only teacher present.

Glore began to say the rules but Roalf interrupted saying, "Okay. We know all the rules. We've heard it twice and that's enough for us. So, can we start to fight?"

"If you're ready."

"We're ready." Roalf said. But I wasn't ready. I was going to fight my geography teacher. Agreed, he is not my teacher now. But I still couldn't take off my impression of Roalf being my favorite teacher. But that wasn't the only reason I didn't want to fight. Roalf was an experienced and a fierce warrior. He was well trained. I was tense.

I didn't speak. I did not say that I wasn't ready. I thought they would think me a coward if I spoke. So I took my usual position, near the lake. Being near water, my confidence rose. I heard Roalf's mocking laugh, "You can attack first."

To prove that I could defeat Roalf easily, I lunged at him. As I swung my sword, he suddenly disappeared. "I'm here." A noise came from above. I recognized it. I looked up and saw Roalf in air smiling at me. Of Course, he was the Lord of Wind. Flying was his natural power.

"Come on," he said.

Now, how was I going to defeat him? He was out of my reach. Neither could I bring him down nor could I fight him. Being the Lord of Wind, Earth was his weakness. Roalf was clever. I had to do something that could bring him down. I thought but came up with nothing.

Spreading my arms I exclaimed sadly, "That's not fair."

Roalf commented giving an old adage, "Everything's fair in love and war."

He was really making me angry. I tightened my grip around my sword. Then Glore said, "I can't help it Alex. Use your brain. You have seven minutes left."

Glore always said that power never mattered in a war and neither did weapons; it was the strategy and determination that mattered. But presently nothing struck me. Nothing came to my mind. I felt blank in my head.

I looked up at Roalf angrily. He launched an arrow at me but I dodged it. Another arrow and I dodged it. Dodging was the only thing that I could do presently. I looked up and then at once a number of arrows were launched at me. They surrounded me completely. I jumped and landed on the ground doing a somersault. The very next second another set of arrows surrounded me. I again jumped and landed. I looked towards the lake. I wasn't near it. But I wasn't too far. If I could just reach it...

But Roalf wasn't going to let me. I really didn't know what to do. I certainly could not give up. I really wanted to win this fight. But how? Again Glore's words saved me. I didn't need a water body for my powers to work. But I just needed a little time to make them work, maybe a second or two...

Then something struck me. An arrow it was. It had pierced my armor. It stung as it touched my skin. Another arrow at my back. Two more at the sides of my waists. What was happening? – I thought. Of which ancient grudge was Roalf feeding fat today?

Suddenly, my survival instincts started working. My fight with Glore was at last going to be useful. Roalf was following the same pattern as Glore. I anticipated the next move. I instantly turned back and hurled my sword aimlessly in the air. It turned out to be in the direction of Roalf. He dodged it. My sword missed him by a whisker.

I held out my hand and the sword returned to me. But Roalf just didn't stop. He continued firing arrows at me. They hit me. Finally I was on my knees. I was raging by the second. I just couldn't control it. Patience has its own limits. But now the limit had been crossed. Blood flowed to my head and my face reddened with anger.

I looked at the mocking face of Roalf. I jumped in the air to cut Roalf on his thigh with the last bit of energy that was left in me and yelled as loudly as I could in blind rage. He disappeared from the spot and my sword missed him. As I had jumped too high in anger I realized that I had to support myself with my sword to avoid landing hard on the ground. I changed my stance midair to point my sword towards the ground and my body perpendicular to it. My sword pierced ground and dug deep into the soil up to the hilt. I fell to the ground with a soft thud. After that I didn't know what happened. I was unconscious.

CHAPTER 17

Anger is your biggest enemy

I opened my eyes. I could see a plain white colored surface without a speck of dirt in front of me. I got up confused. Where was I? I looked around. I was sitting on a beautiful king-sized bed. The bed was in a huge room embellished with flower vases kept in each corner of the room. The windows were covered with curtains of striking design and colors.

I found my sword in its sheath safely resting on the side table. I took it and tried to hang it on the side of my pants...where were my pants! I was wearing a single gown like cloth with cotton trousers. This was not my way of clothing. This was similar to the dressing style of the people of Iregor. Fortunately I wore a belt and so hung my sword by the belt.

The room was neither similar to the one in my house in Iregor nor to that in the Flareds. So where was I? Everything around me seemed royal, from the bed to the flower vases, from the curtains to the shelves in the walls.

I tried to get up rubbing my eyes. Instantly my body flared with pain.. I pulled my shirt up. To my surprise my body bore a number of deep cuts and wounds. My vision turned hazy. My movements were slow, painful and fragile. I felt drowsy and weak. I took a step with difficulty. The second step was a lot of struggle for me. I fell to the ground taking the third step. I realized that I was in no state to move. But why was I in such a state? I wanted answers for all my questions.

I got up once again and took the support of the nearby wall to walk. Gradually, I reached the door and pulled it open. I quit the room and found myself in a corridor with a wooden floor. It stretched a long way right and left. I went up to the hand rail and looked down. On a single sofa set in the middle of a hall sat four figures. I couldn't recognize them due to the blurred vision.

On finding a staircase to my right, I climbed down slowly. I could see a number of chandeliers hanging on the ceiling. They looked similar, and then it struck me. I was in a palace; I was in the Royal Palace. But why? As I reached downstairs I could see the figures more clearly. They were my friends Jack and Jason, Glore and Lord Theromir, the King of Iregor.

Jason noticed me and smiled when I was approaching them. Just then I lost my balance. "Ah!" I exclaimed as I fell. I heard footsteps rushing towards me. A second later I was lifted tenderly. I could feel the hands of Jack and Jason under my head and legs. I felt the warm touch of the sofa as they laid me there. I think they had been conversing; apparently I had broken their conversation.

Jason and Jack sat beside me. I could read concern in their faces. As for Glore and Lord Theromir, without a doubt they were concerned too. It took me a while to open my mouth, but when I did I felt much better. The drowsiness was fading and I felt relaxed.

"What happened to me and why are we here?" I asked.

Jason answered me in a shower of hurried words as if he had to leave to attend some important business. "When I and Jack were fighting, we heard a loud noise, sounding like an explosion, coming from the neighboring room in which you and Roalf were fighting."

"Wait a minute," I interrupted, "what are these fights and the loud noise?"

"Don't tell me Alex that you remember nothing about the fights and your training with Glore," Jack said. It took me a while to recollect the recent past. And then everything fell into place - from my training with Glore to the fights with Jack, Jason and Roalf. But I felt that something was missing about my fight with Roalf; something I couldn't remember.

"So we abandoned our fight and rushed to your room. When we entered it we saw that you and Roalf were lying on the ground with your sword dug deep into the ground. Glore was running between you and Roalf worried. But we don't know what actually happened," Jason stopped there.

Jack continued for him saying, "Glore would never tell us. We pleaded with him, but he wouldn't tell."

"So will you tell me Glore?" I asked him.

"No, I cannot. It's too dangerous for you", he answered.

Dissatisfied I asked, "In what way?"

"It might make you fear your own powers," Glore said shuddering a little.

"I see." I said disbelieving. I sensed that Glore wasn't going to speak further on the topic. Something was different about him. He didn't look relaxed and cool as he was before. He seemed worried and tensed. I wanted to get to the bottom of this case. But I hastily changed the topic.

"What happened to me?" I asked, "Why do I feel so weak?"

"You fell unconscious at that time. You had a couple of arrows pierced through your armor and a couple of them in your thighs." Jack answered, "You feel weak because you're exhausted. It's been three days and still you haven't gained back your energy."

The last line spoken by Jack bewildered me. I couldn't believe what I heard. It has been three days and I still feel exhausted. I instantly felt thirsty. "I needed water." A glass of water was kept on the centre table. I immediately picked it up and emptied the glass. I felt a bit relaxed.

On realizing the absence of Roalf, I asked, "Where's Roalf?"

"He's in his room, sleeping." The King of Iregor spoke.

"Is he alright?"

"Um...he's actually sort of sick," he said stammering.

"What!" I was astonished, "What did I do to him?"

"Don't worry Alex. He's alright. He'll be okay in a week as told by the doctor," Glore said trying to calm me.

"I want to see him," I said, "Where is he?"

"Relax, Alex. Go and rest now. I'll take you to Roalf in the evening." Glore said.

"Okay."

"And Alex," Glore called.

"Yes, Glore?"

"Remember, anger is your biggest enemy. You have to learn to control your anger." He said it with much concern for me but I did not understand why he said that to me. I didn't find it significant at that time. Nodding to Glore, I returned to my room upstairs and fell into a deep sleep as soon as I hit the bed.

I opened my eyes and found myself lying on wet ground amidst a few trees and bushes. Was I in a forest? But how? I should be in my room in the Royal Palace of Iregor. Okay, this is a dream. I got up (in my dream) and walked to figure out where I actually was. The moonlight lit my way. It was raining and I liked nothing better than rain.

This forest looked completely different from the Bulkite forest. I thanked my fate that I hadn't ended up there in my dream. After walking for a while the forest ended and a river burst out at a distance from me. It must have come from the forest. I found myself on the top of a hill. I walked further on a downward sloping land. Yells, battle cries and noise of explosions filled the air. The air had a foul smell. I wondered what was going on.

Then suddenly my eyes fell on the battle scene. It was astonishing, horrible, disgusting and whatever adjectives you might add to it. It looked like the aftermath of mixing of a huge ratio of two dirty chemicals in a big test tube to give a reversible exothermic reaction with an explosion and a loud noise.

The atmosphere was awful. I ran to the middle of the battleground anticipating that no one would attack me. I could now easily make out the two different armies fighting; one was that of men and the other one of tall dirty looking smelly beings. Maybe they were Giants but I hope not.

Swords clashed, spears broke, heads rolled and blood spurted out. Everything was pretty horrifying. But I had no reason to be scared as all this was only a dream and I had my sword with me. Then I saw him, a young handsome looking man with a sharp nose and long hair, thick eyebrows and blue green eyes yelling orders with his sword raised and fighting hordes of dirty looking beasts. His sword was a long sharp one which glowed in the moonlight. But I couldn't place him in my memory.

Then the armies separated; mankind to the left and the dirty looking to the right. I realized that they were regrouping. "Sior! Lead the left flank. Leon! Lead the right flank. Roalf! Stay with me." I heard the man say. So the ones standing with the man were Jack's father – the Lord of Earth, Jason's father – the Lord of Fire and Roalf – my ex-geography teacher and the Lord of Wind.

"No Dane we cannot continue fighting like this," The Lord of Earth spoke, his voice a sharp one, "the Giants are regrouping in large numbers." Okay, so all doubts cleared; the dirty looking beasts are the Giants and the handsome man is my father, the Lord of Water - Dane.

"Sior's right," Leon spoke, "we need to find their hideous king. That unearthly beast." That meant Maut. Just then I felt some commotion to my right. The Giants had parted to make way. Not a sound in the air. Slowly I heard heavy footsteps with the clinking of metal. And then I saw it, the most dreadful being I had ever seen in my life. A twenty feet monster with a fat belly having large round eyes, huge ears that had grown forward like blinkers on a horse, and three horns on his head. The horns themselves were as tall as I was, with the middle one being taller. His skin was twisted and scaled and had a faint glow of green and blue. He carried a strong scent of garlic that was too pungent to bear. He held a sceptre in his right hand which had a large unblemished ruby fixed into it. Emerald colored spikes rose all over his body. Some penetrated his magnificent crown, some were present on his horns too. Maybe he had a lust for precious stones. This creature was Maut, the very same monster in my previous dream.

I saw the Lords run toward Maut with their weapons raised. And then all the four weapons clashed with the sceptre of Maut. Nothing happened. Then the Lords surrounded Maut from all sides and pierced his huge body all over. It was obviously hurting the Giant King and he shrieked in pain. Angrily the Giant yelled and banged his sceptre on the ground. All sound and light ceased except that of the radiant ruby. The next second, light returned and I could see that both the armies were reduced to half their size.

"Oh my God!" I thought. What magic! What evil! I don't know whether the Lords were hurt but they were certainly knocked off their feet. The Giant walked up to them. He stood there laughing. But I think I saw something in orange - red, like fire. And I was right. Leon's spear hit Maut's face. Maut instantly backed down rubbing his eyes. And then I saw that from the ground a twisting green stem with thorns and leaves was growing and wrapping itself around the Giant's body. That may be Sior. I saw Roalf jump in the air pushing his hands downwards. Instantly the sceptre was knocked out of the hand of Maut, maybe by the wind.

And then I saw my father tap his right foot from under which came a shower of water directed towards Maut's face blurring his vision. But I could clearly see that King Dane had, in a swift movement, cut the sceptre into two— the one with the ruby in his hand and the staff lying on the ground.

I opened my eyes. I wasn't really surprised by the dream. Since the previous dream I always expected another to come. But I didn't understand what this dream was all about. The Lords were fighting the Giant

King Maut. As per our history books, the Lords fought Maut only once and that was in the grounds of Gorum. So it was evident that my dream depicted the Battle of Gorum.

I got up. To my surprise Jason was sitting on a chair beside the bed. "Hi Jason."

"So you are up. How do you feel now?" He asked smiling.

"Better," I replied.

"Yeah. You look much better."

"Thanks. What's the time?"

"It's six in the evening." He said looking at his watch.

"I want to see Roalf. Where is he?"

"I'll take you to him. Jack and Glore are waiting for us there."

I got out of the bed and Jason led me out of the room. It was easier for me to walk now. The drowsiness that I felt earlier was gone. We took some lefts and rights, some stairs and then finally reached Roalf's room.

My heart was pounding. I wished that Roalf was fine. I knocked on the door and waited. Jack opened it. He smiled on seeing me and Jason. "Come on in", he said.

I saw Glore sitting beside a bed. The bed had a white bed sheet and a white blanket between which lay the thin body of Roalf dressed in green-colored clothes. The room looked like one in a hospital. I was concerned for Roalf. I couldn't think of a reason for Roalf to be in such a state.

Jack pulled me to a chair beside the bed. I sat on it. I bent forward and held Roalf's hand. It was weak and thin. I felt the pulse. The pulse rate was low. Roalf turned towards me with his eyes open. He gave me a smile that was the brightest I had ever seen.

"How are you Roalf?" I asked softly.

"I'm good...I'm recovering fast." He replied. His voice was frail and he coughed frequently. It was really saddening to see Roalf in such a state. I was silent.

"By the way I was really amazed by your power that day. It was like seeing Dane fight his enemy. I was up in the air flying till you managed to bring me down. Excellent Alex, good work." He said.

I didn't know what to say.

Roalf then coiled up into a sleeping position and closed his eyes. My eyes were moist. The guilt of bringing Roalf into such a state made me feel weak. I got up and went so close to Glore that it was enough to scare him.

"What did I do to him?" I asked gravely.

"Alex -" He began but I interrupted him.

"What did I do to him?" This time raising my voice a little. There came no reply.

Frustrated I cried, "**WHAT DID I DO TO HIM?**"

"You almost killed him! Is that Okay? Does that satisfy you?" Glore shouted back.

That was too much for me to bear. I could not carry the weight of the guilt. To find out how I almost killed

Roalf I rushed toward the room where Roalf and I were fighting.

I would never forgive myself for this. I was the reason for Roalf's present condition. But I had to figure out how. My conscience throbbed with pain. My exceptional concentration and mental outlook had been disturbed. My confidence had been completely shattered.

Even at a fast pace it took me a while to reach my destination. The palace was a big one. It had a number of gardens and ballrooms.

My steps slowed down as I reached the room. I opened it and entered and banged the door shut behind me. There was not a change in the room. Even the playground in which I and Roalf fought was there. There was no alteration in the landscape. However, I felt that something was missing.

As I neared it, my eye caught something. I stopped dead...the trough in which the lake was contained was empty showing only the lake bed. I entered the playground. It was wet. The soil had turned into mud. I did not understand. As I moved to the center I saw a deep hole in the ground. It was at least a foot deep. So there was a change in the landscape. To understand what this was all about I sat down thinking.

I went through all my memories of the fight. I remembered how Roalf had launched arrows at me, how he had made me fall to the ground with the arrows penetrating my armor and skin. It really was painful. I remembered his mocking laugh. I remembered how

Roalf fooled me by launching arrows at my upper body from all different directions. I remembered how I'd hurled my sword in the direction of Roalf and how it had missed him by a whisker. I remembered the taunting face of Roalf.

I remembered how... Wait a minute; I don't remember anything after that. But how's that possible, the fight could not be over at the point because Glore had said that I'd almost killed Roalf. So what was the missing part? I'd to figure it out, somehow.

There had to be some hint. The empty lake, the wet ground, the deep hole...there had to be a connection. What could it be? I assumed all these as hints. Then I merged these hints with my memories of the fight. And then everything fitted in, everything made sense. Yes, it did.

After I'd hurled my sword in Roalf's direction, I had jumped high in the air in anger and then dug my sword into the ground (the hole looked of that made by my sword) expecting to protect myself from the fall. Nevertheless some magical event had occurred. My sword must have sucked all the water in the lake to the sword hole from underground and blasted the water mass toward Roalf hurting him severely. He must have been out of breath for a while unable to escape the rapid jet. Naturally, I must have fallen unconscious because I had used up all of my energy.

I got up and first filled the surrounding mud into the hole. I had the objective of converting the wet playground as it was before because I did not want to remember this fight. It had filled me with guilt. I then walked up to the centre of the empty trough. If my sword could channelize all the water in the lake to the hole, then it could obviously channelize all the water back into the trough.

I brought my sword out and touched the centre of the trough with its tip. Gradually but steadily all the water returned to the lake from the wet ground. Again, no problem in breathing underwater. I walked out of the lake in dry clothes and put the sword back into its sheath. The wet ground had turned dry again.

I'd finally got the answer to my question. The answer had increased my confidence to a greater level as it told me that I had immense power but it also filled me with guilt. Nonetheless the answer taught me something new. I walked out of the room remembering Glore's words – *"ANGER IS YOUR BIGGEST ENEMY"*.

CHAPTER 18

Quite a lot happens

Many weeks passed since the fights. I did not work much, Glore wouldn't allow me. I was still very thin, but I was gradually gaining weight. Roalf was recovering too and I was happy with the development. I used to visit him frequently although I never met his eyes because I still bore the guilt. It stuck to me like a magnet.

It had been weeks since Jason and Jack had left Iregor and they hadn't returned yet from Ferogor and Garyland. I'd started to get bored without them. Ferogor was the birth place of Jason's father and Garyland was the birthplace of Jack's father.

"It all happened on the spur of the moment." Glore would tell me. I hadn't known until they had already left. I hadn't even known when they had planned everything. It all happened one day when I was in my quarters sleeping. I was woken up by Lord Theromir's loud laughter. I looked down through the window. The window overlooked one of the Royal Gardens in the

Palace. In the garden I spotted four figures laughing and conversing together with a number of soldiers.

On straining my eyes I saw Jack and Jason, and Glore and Lord Theromir. Jack and Jason were well dressed and had backpacks as if they were going somewhere on an adventure.

Just then I saw Glore raise his hand. The action was followed by the formation of a portal in front of Jack and Jason. I wondered what was going on. I hurried out of my room, climbed downstairs and took several rights and lefts to reach the garden. Alas! Jack and Jason had already left with the soldiers. When I asked Lord Theromir and Glore about where Jack and Jason had gone, Glore told me that they had left for Garyland and Ferogor.

"Why?" I had asked.

Lord Theromir answered me, "We will tell that to you when they return with news. Now go and rest." As it was impossible for me to disobey the king, I simply returned to my room thinking about the portal.

A year had passed since the start of our adventure and I'd practically forgotten everything about Fymland. I was no more the shy and introvert boy who always scored less marks in exams. Nor was I the boy who used to bear banters from Mrs. Philips. I was simply Alex, son of King Dane and Lord of Water who wielded the Holy Sword of Iregor. I undoubtedly missed the delicious, juicy grapes of Fymland but that couldn't change my objective of destroying the ruby. No matter what happened I had to continue with my quest.

A number of parties and feasts were held in the palace. The king had no guests from outside Iregor. And hardly anybody left Iregor. If someone did, the king was informed. And then the traveler had to vow that he wouldn't share the secrets of Iregor with anyone. The king would then dispatch some soldiers to ensure the traveler's safety and also to ensure that he keeps his vow. After my description, Iregor might look like a prison to you. But the Iregorians very well knew that it was for their own good that the king did all this. Iregor was frequently attacked by Giants, Glore had told me once. All these actions of the King ensured Iregor's safety.

Clarus, the king's son would visit me frequently to check on my health. All this time, during the absence of my friends, Clarus would take care of me as if he were my brother. He would accompany me anywhere I wished to go within the palace premises. He sort of acted like a bodyguard and a dear friend.

As for Lord Theromir, he would always stay with his brother. He would never leave the room until some important business needed him. Roalf's every wish was anticipated and carried out cheerfully. With Lord Theromir's and Clarus' constant support and love, it was not long before we recovered completely.

A week passed this way, Roalf and I had fully recovered. I was once again the active and strong boy who wasn't scared of anything. But there was still no news from Jack and Jason.

"When are they going to come back?" I asked, "I'm getting worried." Glore, Roalf and I were sitting around a table having fresh milk and nuts.

"They'll come. Don't worry." Glore would calm me.

"But what is taking them so long?" I asked.

"May be the people of Garyland and Ferogor are not allowing them to leave. I remember the places very well." Roalf said, "When Dane and I had visited these places for the first time, the folks were mad with joy at seeing us and made us live there for six months. Maybe Jack and Jason are also facing the same situation. After all it is the homeland of their fathers."

"But I want to see them," I pleaded.

"Okay." Glore said. He moved his hand touching the sphere of his staff with his eyes closed. The green hue turned white and then it projected a picture in air. I saw Jack and Jason being cheerfully carried by a mob of people. The people were smiling and yelling something which I couldn't hear. That meant they were screaming with joy. A strong temptation of visiting my friends arose in me.

"Jack and Jason are in Ferogor. They are already done with Garyland. Great."

"Does that mean that they'll be back soon?" Roalf asked.

"Yes," Glore answered.

Just then the picture vanished and the green hue returned. "There," Glore said, "Are you happy now?"

"Yes...but can I visit them?" I asked speaking slowly.

"Now, now, I know where you're getting. King Theromir has strictly ordered that you both should not leave the palace. Forget leaving Iregor."

"Please Glore. Only for a while. No one will know," I pleaded.

"No!" He said.

"Please," I pleaded again putting up an innocent face.

"Okay. But only for ten minutes."

"Thank you Glore," I said smiling.

"You'd better go with him, Roalf. I cannot trust a kid on serious matters." My cheeks reddened on being considered a kid but at least Glore had allowed me to go. So I didn't react.

He raised his hand and instantly there appeared a portal. "You've got ten minutes. The portal will remain open for you to return. You better be back before the portal closes. Your time starts now." I entered the portal followed by Roalf.

On the other side, there was a completely different world. I'd ended up dashing two soldiers standing on a stage. When we separated they raised their spears on us. On recognizing me and Roalf, they instantly lowered their spears and their heads. I glared at them. I spotted a river ten meters away from the stage.

I turned my attention to the crowd. No one had noticed us. In the center of the mob I spotted my friends. They were being carried by the crowd. I could see their happy faces. I advanced to the end of the stage and called out, "Jack, Jason. Hey, it's me Alex."

They couldn't hear me. I tried once again but in vain. This time I shouted louder, louder than the crowd's screaming, "**JACK, JASON**?"

The crowd put them down. They turned their heads towards me and Roalf. A big smile crossed their lips and they ran on to the stage hugging me and Roalf one by one.

"How are you?" Jason asked.

"I'm fine," I and Roalf replied in unison.

"Oh man, you look smatter and fatter. Congrats." Jack regarded me.

"Thanks."

"And Roalf looks like Mr. Thomas. Congrats to you too." Jack said.

"Jason seems very happy," Roalf said.

"Yes. This is my father's birthplace. It is beautiful." Jason said that with happiness. I smiled.

"By the way," He turned to the crowd, "This is Alex, the Lord of Water and this is Roalf, the Lord of Wind." It had been quite some time since I'd exercised my powers and so I was excited and in a mood to show off as much as I could.

I jumped off the stage and ran towards the river. Tensed, some people followed me. As I neared the river I jumped and removed my sword in a swift action in midair and then willed the water to rise up so that I could have a base to stand. I did all this in a split second.

Sounds cool. I know. But it was not as easy as it sounded like. However, I managed. I stood there, on pure liquid water, pointing my sword to the sky. I was pretty good at giving heroic poses.

The crowd stared at me dazed. They had the look on their faces that seemed to say, *"Dude! That's too much for us to see"*. I stood there for a few seconds and then jumped down. The crowd rushed towards me. It looked like they were coming to kill me. But they were coming to pick me up. That sounded fun.

I was beaming with joy when the mob picked me up. I had felt such happiness after a long time. I looked up at the sky. The Sun was shining bright. I think I saw a line divide the Sun into two halves…or was it an arrow. Yes, it was an arrow. I saw plenty of them passing in a second. One needed much accuracy for doing that thing and the only person with such caliber I knew was Roalf.

Plenty of them passed my eyes. It looked as if they were forming words. After a few seconds the words were completed.

They read: Hello Ferogor

That was simply amazing. And I wasn't wrong. It was Roalf. An image of him high up in the air with his bow crossed my eyes. All the arrows returned to his quiver that hung on his back. The bow and the quiver disappeared and the next moment he was on the ground.

A moment later he was joyfully lifted up by a group of people. The crowd slowly set us standing on the stage. They were cheering for me and Roalf. I turned back and the portal was still there but it was smaller now.

I heard a man speak; the voice was not of my friends'. "You've changed a lot Roalf." I turned back and saw an old man dressed in royal clothes hug Roalf tightly.

"I know," Roalf answered.

When they separated, the man said bowing, "My apologies for talking to you like that, my Lord. King Forman at your service." So it was King Forman who had spoken. It sounded pretty weird; I'd never heard Roalf being called as "Lord" except for the people of Iregor.

"No, my Lord. It's not you who should be bowing. Roalf is at your service." Roalf said generously and bowed.

I did the same. "Alex, at your service."

I turned to Jack and Jason who had been smiling all the time and said, "We must leave now...no questions. Glore had given us ten minutes. Goodbye and make haste. We await you in the palace of Iregor."

Jason spoke, "We'll be back in a day's time. That's our promise."

I turned towards the crowd and said goodbye. Those guys out there were so affectionate. I really loved those guys. I turned back and left Ferogor through the portal, which was diminishing quickly now, followed by Roalf.

I met Glore on the other side sitting by the round table. "Just in time," he said. I turned back and saw the portal diminish into a single speck. Roalf stood beside me.

"Those guys are so cool," I said. "We enjoyed a lot."

"Yeah, I saw everything." Glore said.

The next day our little company including me, Roalf, Lord Theromir and Glore sat on a sofa set having breakfast awaiting Jack and Jason's return. Just then a portal opened up beside Lord Theromir, and out of it jumped Jack and Jason and a few soldiers who immediately left.

"Hullo," Jack said, "We've brought good news."

King Theromir exclaimed drily, "Unfortunately you both are no harbingers."

They sat down beside me and started talking. "Both Garyland and Ferogor have accepted our invitation for war with the Giants." Jason said.

"Can you please explain your story from the start?" I asked as I hadn't understood the background to what Jason had spoken.

After much talking I understood everything. In the absence of me and Roalf, Jack, Jason, Glore and Lord Theromir had had a meeting in which they had discussed about the final war that would be the climax of our quest.

Glore had told that the Giants were in huge numbers and their population was increasing every year. In that case the army of Iregor would be outnumbered. So to be on the safe side Glore had suggested that nothing was wrong in asking Garyland and Ferogor for help. He had said this on the understanding that the war would decide the fate of the world and so Garyland and Ferogor had to take part. Glore had felt that Garyland and Ferogor would agree for sure and accept our invitation because we, the Lords are going to lead them in war.

"But why not Fymland?" I asked, "It is also their responsibility to take part in the war."

"Yes it is. But we already know that Fymland would not help because they don't believe that lands like Iregor still exist. And they are also very different from us. People have become selfish there. It's no use to go there and invite them." Glore answered me.

Disappointed, I fell silent. But I knew that Glore was right in his place. People in Fymland were really selfish as they believed in modern day capitalism. And they also strongly believed that there were no lands in the west. I would *now* call that extreme egotism.

An atmosphere of interest and mystery prevailed for a while. Everyone was lost in thoughts. Jack and Jason would frequently reach out to the tart and jam tray. They were hungry. It was well understood.

Travelling through portals takes a lot out of you. I've always felt hungry after every portal travel. Portal travel may sound pretty awesome. But believe me, it's not just that and it's not at all easy. Portal travel is not like entering a doorway and saying "wow", I am at my destination. It has a doorway and another side. Agreed. But after you enter it, it's like travelling at a high speed. Even that makes you exhausted. It does make your head spin and your stomach empty. Continuous portal travel can even cause death.

The words of a guard brought us back to reality from our thoughts. "My lord, Elvin, the blacksmith has come to see you all."

"Send him," the King replied. The guard departed with the order. A few minutes later an old man was escorted towards us by a guard. He had a short beard and a small nose. His skin was wrinkled and veins were showing on his hand. This showed that he worked too much and ate little.

He bowed before the King and nodded to Glore. "Here I present to you Elvin Rings, one of the blacksmiths who forged the ruby. He'll be your guide for tomorrow when you visit the Egor Mountains." Glore said.

By 8 a.m. the next day, we, the Lords were on the banks of Egorian River accompanied by Elvin Rings. A weird name, but suited him very well. Maybe he had a liking for rings. Indeed he wore a ring on each of his fingers on both his hands.

We boarded a large boat that would take us to the base of the Egor Mountains. A large number of rowers accompanied us. For the first time in my life, I was standing on a boat. It felt very nice. I had the feeling as if the whole world was under my control.

After a few try outs, I realized that being the Lord of water I could control the speed of the boat. That was fun. Sometimes I made the boat speed quickly. The rowers got scared and thought that wind was playing tricks. And then I would slow down the boat completely. The rowers were confused and thought the boat had a mind of its own.

It really felt nice to be on a water body. The air around and the smell of water, everything seemed like a song. The greatest thing about the rivers of Iregor is that they are pristine. There was no water pollution in the rivers. I could sense that. There was plenty of aquatic life in the water.

It was not long before we reached the base of the Mountains. I alighted the boat. Five horses stood at the base. I guessed they were for us. I went up to them.

The men guarding the horses were quick to recognize us. We had become famous in Iregor. The king had made sure that every single man knew us. His men had stuck posters bearing our faces at every wall in the kingdom.

We mounted the horses. A single road wound up the mountain taking many sharp curves. I looked up. Up and up the mountain went tapering as it went northwards and then disappeared into the clouds. Now, I could even see the dark patch which was probably in the middle. I never had a problem with heights but now I was a little scared.

I kicked my horse lightly and it went up the road. I'd never learnt horse riding and doing it now was amazing. Jack did it as if it came naturally to him. Of course, he blends with nature's every gift. He was scared of heights, I knew that. Still he tried to hide his fear. I hadn't even spoken a word to the old man, Elvin Rings. Roalf and Elvin spoke as if they were old friends. He was one of the blacksmiths who had forged the ruby. Strange, he's alive. The thing that I never understood was that why did the ruby need to be forged knowing that it was evil.

We cantered on the mountain track. It took us time to reach our destination. I didn't know what it was. Glore only told us that we were going to visit the Egor Mountains. We stopped all at once at Elvin's command. Beside us a dark cave could be seen. It really freaked me out. Oh! Man, I had had enough of darkness in my life.

"We have to go in there." Elvin spoke. His voice was croaky.

It occurred to me that the ground on which I was standing had a very dark hue, almost black. Everything in and about this place almost looked as if they were covered by a shadow. I asked Roalf, "Why is this place so dark? It's very grave and gloomy." Elvin answered for Roalf.

"After we had forged the ruby, there was a big explosion here, many died. This is an after effect of the explosion. It looks like a dark patch from afar." Then it struck me what that dark patch actually was.

We followed Elvin into the cave. There was complete darkness. Jason brought fire onto his hand.

"No need for that." The old man said. Elvin picked a torch that hung on the side wall by means of a hook. He lowered the torch into Jason's fire and it immediately caught fire. "Now extinguish that." He said rudely. Jason raised his eyebrows and looked at me. He closed his fist and the fire vanished.

After much walking we stopped. We had come to a dead end. The wall ahead was made of bricks. Elvin stepped forward and drew some pattern of vertical and horizontal lines and diagonals. A rumbling sound could be heard that was a result of the brick wall moving towards the right revealing a hidden chamber. It didn't freak me out. I had seen enough of them. There must be some mechanism.

A podium kind of a thing, made of black rocks could be seen in the centre and had a depression on its top surface. The whole chamber was not so big. Some axes and hammers lay in a corner.

"This is the place where the ruby was forged. I and my companions worked long and hard with scarcely any rest for a year in this secret chamber. No one knew about it except us and the King at that time." Elvin said.

"I don't understand why the ruby needed to be forged knowing that it was evil." I dropped in.

"It needed to be forged because of the wishes of King Bor, the father of Lord Theromir and Lord Roalf." Elvin said that with such distaste that it was immediately understood that he had been forced to forge the ruby. The answer shocked everyone.

Roalf raised his eyebrows. "No, that cannot be true. My father lived only for the people. He was not evil."

"But he was selfish. Mark my words; selfishness is a prime evil in the world. It is a chief sin. King Bor wanted to take over this world. The ruby is only a precious stone. But it was forged out of immense selfishness and so it became a weapon of mass destruction."

"Who were your companions?" Jason asked.

"Blacksmiths just like me. But...," he stopped speaking.

I encouraged him, "Yes, go on."

"But one of them was a Giant."

"What!" We were shocked.

"No my father would not work with Giants." Roalf said. He just couldn't believe his ears and neither could I. His face had grown pale and expressionless. The secrets of his father had pretty much dumbfounded him.

"He was not a normal Giant. He was a good one, the greatest blacksmith the world has ever known. His name was Jargon. King Bor had caught him wandering in the Bulkite forests. King Bor had realized Jargon's worth. With Jargon, forging a weapon of mass destruction had become easier. But we could not let the world sink into evil. Jargon cut a small part of the ruby and then remolded the left over ruby into proper shape."

He continued, "But we needed something which had immense positive energy. We found that positive energy in King Dane's sword. No one knew how Dane's sword was forged and by whom. After his death, Glore brought it to us. But Jargon had been captured by Maut. He had taken Jargon with him. Nevertheless his ideas were with us. We molded the part of the ruby with Dane's sword. It finally became the Holy Sword of Iregor."

"Which is this," I said and unsheathed my sword.

"Yes. I suppose Glore gave it to you?" Elvin said unaffected.

Just then a portal opened up behind Elvin. Glore's head popped out of it, "Hurry everyone, we have had

an attack from the Giants. Hurry, we don't have time."
Saying that the portal closed.

We stood there for a few moments worried. I was
angry at Glore for not leaving the portal for us but I had
no time to think over my emotions. We dashed out of
the cave. I jumped and mounted my horse. I did this for
the first time in my life and without success. I was about
to fall when Jack caught me and put me back onto the
horse properly. I kicked it hard in anxiety. It ran down
the mountain like a mad dog.

We reached the river in no time. I jumped and
dashed into the river and started swimming at top speed
while Jack continued to ride on the horse. Roalf was
flying at top speed and Jason...Oh my god, Jason was
flying too. His hands were stuck to his body but his
palm was open. His whole body was glowing and fire
shot out of his palms and legs. Looking at him was like
seeing a rocket launch.

Okay, no time for personification. We reached the
market in no time. But unfortunately it was too late. The
view that we saw bowled us over. Shops were on fire.
Men, women and children were lying on the ground.
Patches of blood covered the clean streets of the market.
Some who were alive were badly injured and ran helter-
skelter. Tables and banners were fallen. Glore stood by
a broken down shop. King Theromir was sitting with
his head in his hands.

We walked to Glore and Lord Theromir. People
gathered around us. The king got up, restored his
persona and addressed his people. He encouraged them

to have trust in the Lords and promised that they would have their revenge.

"It is an inside job," I got up and spoke to the desolate Iregorians, "There is a traitor. How did the giants know the secret to enter Iregor?"

I was going to open my mouth to speak had not my eyes caught movement towards the left. On a roof of a house a figure draped in black clothes was silently getting away. Maybe he was the traitor. I secretly addressed Roalf, "Roalf take me to that roof."

He picked me up and flew over to the roof. But the traitor had taken notice of me. He ran jumping from roof to roof. He was fast but I caught up with him. My sword clashed with his armor. I performed various combos but all were blocked. My opponent's movements were quick but I held my ground. I realized that he was a fierce warrior.

He pushed me down on the roof. He tried thrusting a long knife into my chest but I blocked his attempt. Our weapons clashed and sparks flew. I tried to rise but he was pushing me down. Finally I kicked him in the groin and he retreated. He stumbled over the edge of the roof and fell onto the public street. I jumped down.

My opponent's face was covered by a hood. I pulled the hood back just enough to reveal a dirty, nose less grey face with ears like that of a monkey's. I was beholding the face of a Giant who was too short compared to others of his kin. He had only one foot on each of his legs unlike the other Giants and he did not smell garlic nor his skin glowed green and blue during exertion. It seemed like the Giant's mutation had stopped abruptly. I pointed my sword at his face. The mob gasped.

Lord Theromir approached me and gasped too, "A giant?" He said with an astonished but a furious voice.

"Why are you here?" He asked the Giant ferociously, "How do you know about the secrets of Iregor?"

But the Giant wouldn't answer. It (or he, I'm confused about which pronoun I should use for a Giant) kept mum. I brought my sword closer to his chin.

"Don't answer. Fine." The king shouted, "May be you're an Iregorian who turned into a Giant. I don't know about its possibility but that can be the only reason for your knowledge of our secrets. I charge you with treason! Alex kill it!"

I raised my sword in a swift action. The mini Giant closed his eyes.

"Please, my Lord, don't kill him!"

I straightened myself and even the creature opened its eyes astonished. I saw that on a hairy white horse sat the blacksmith Elvin Rings. Jack was furious at him. "But why? It's because of this beast that the Giants were able to attack us. Why should we not kill it?"

The answer that Elvin gave made us speechless, "Because, it is but for this Giant that you've got a chance of destroying the ruby of Ganohan."

CHAPTER 19

Jargon instructs

The attack on the market was of great significance to the King. It had been a great imbroglio – whether to let the giant live or not. Weeks had passed since the attack and still Lord Theromir hadn't come out of his grieving for his people killed. But he was at his best agility because the decision he was to take needed thinking twice over.

He had sent spies to look out if any of the Giants were snooping outside Iregor. Apparently the mini Giant whom I had fought in the market had turned out to be Jargon. The King had mostly avoided the blacksmith and had treated him very rudely. But he had immediately felt sorry when came to know the pigmy Giant's accomplishments. It was not long before the pigmy Giant was begun to be respected in the whole country of Iregor.

The pigmy Giant usually remained quiet. It rarely opened its mouth but when it did, it was like hearing a snake speak. His voice trailed off in a series of hisses and words. Whenever it had encountered the King (before the King's view of it changed), a war of expressions of hatred could be seen.

The pigmy seemed to mix with no one except Elvin Rings. They behaved as if they were old friends. Since the pigmy had become a person of national importance and was called by name - Jargon, the palace had become its home and so the King had to shift Elvin Rings to the palace as well.

Jargon too avoided people but he became supremely different when he started receiving respect from them. He would even greet people when he met them on the road. The greeting would be returned back with a sweet, respectful voice without any hesitation. His chest would usually puff up with pride.

Even my friends including Glore had got on with him as well. But I could not do so. My hatred for the Giants persisted even in the case of Jargon. I did not like him; consequently I avoided him. But I found that I could not continue doing so. He always used to pop out of somewhere. It seemed as if he used to follow me. The more I thought of this, the less I liked him but he seemed to be there everywhere.

He always used to try to make me talk. Sometimes he would say, "It's a very pleasant morning." I would ignore him and move ahead when he said the second sentence.

"It was very bad of my kin to attack the market."

I was tempted to smash his face and say, "Yeah, it was very bad of you dirty, smelling beasts to kill our people! Thanks for the sympathy but we really don't need it!" But I could only manage to say, "Ye...Yeah"

A cruel, mocking smile had spread on his face. And then all of a sudden it had died.

"You think we are bad, don't you," he had asked. I did not reply.

He continued, "I'd asked myself the same question, are we bad? Nevertheless I had got the disheartening reply: Yes. But actually we aren't. We are the same as you all, Alex. No creature is born evil. We become evil, due to selfishness and lust for power. Everybody follows their King, in our case King Maut. But then why am I not evil, if Giants are? Because I don't care for power. I do not need power. I am alright with a simple life. You know Alex, my experiences hold me from turning bad. People fall in mysterious ways. Even King Maut has children and do you think that he behaves rudely with them. No, he is as generous to his people as Lord Theromir is. I have lived for complete two hundred years and I fail to see an end to my life. You think lords are only born in human race. But about two hundred years ago four Lord Giants were born and it happened before them too. We are all connected Alex. We are different only superficially but internally we are the same. We just have a different way of living. I hope you will think over this. Your conduct with me has really been bad. It has hurt me."

Since that day, the words of Jargon had always been ringing in my ears. I couldn't believe what he had said but I still knew that it was true.

Jargon had told us his story. It seemed that he completely trusted us. After Jargon had been captured by Maut, he was directly taken to Ganohan where he was charged with treason but was not put to death. He was tortured to reveal all the secrets of Iregor. Naturally he had to blurt out everything he knew. Maut had shown some sympathy on him because of his being a Giant, though a pigmy. After he was discharged from prison he was again made the royal blacksmith. His respect had been restored.

During Jargon's time in prison Maut had snatched the ruby from Iregor. His wife and children had all died in the Battle of Gorum. That was too much for him. He had hoped that someday this would all end. Fate had it that Iregor was several times attacked but Jargon had had no chance of escape from the Giants. Fortunately this time when the Giants were returning after they had finished the attack no one had taken any notice of him. Silently he had hid himself behind a shop, draped in black clothes which he had found on a street.

He had done so because he had felt bad for the people of Iregor and he wanted to help them. He was successful in escaping and was moving silently upon roofs in search of shelter. But I had noticed him and had immediately taken him down. When I had pointed my sword towards him he had been astonished. That had been a shock to him. He had recognized my sword immediately, its blue aura. He had been happy to die at that moment believing that good would take over evil and that the ruby would be destroyed.

But just then he had heard someone plead for him. This too was a shock for him. That was Elvin Rings. He was very happy that he had found someone whom he could completely trust. He had also realized that he could trust the human world just as he could trust his kin.

He was proud of himself to walk in a street without hiding his face. Jargon promised us that he would try his best to help us destroy the ruby. He had felt obliged to do so. He also said that there was a chance of destroying the ruby for sure but it entirely depended on the Lords. He said that the Giants' army was growing in numbers every year and that Iregor needed a bigger army. But Glore assured him that preparations for a big army had been made as Ferogor and Garyland were also joining the war that was close at hand.

After Jargon had told his story, King Theromir was confident of his decision of fighting the war. Now he felt almost certain that we would finish off the Giants.

Somehow I had started to like Jargon. I had become more open with him. The next day we had again visited the cave. We had done this upon Jargon's request. The journey to the cave was the same. First the boat, then the horses and finally to the cave.

We came to the brick wall inside the cave. Jargon moved his hands in the same way as Elvin had. The wall moved right with a rumbling sound revealing the hidden cavern. The rock podium stood in the center with its depression shining black. It had given me an eerie feeling when I had first come here and it gave me that feeling now too.

The entire cavern was very depressing. It smelled as if something was burning. I certainly did not like it.

Jargon moved in a circle around the podium touching it. He then moved his hands towards the depression and closed his eyes as if he was trying to reminisce what had happened there. Then he spoke in the same hissing tone:

"In order to destroy the ruby, it is very important for you to know how to destroy it.

We kept quiet, so he continued, "The evil weapon can only be destroyed in the place where it was forged. That means it can only be destroyed right here, in this cave in the Egor Mountains."

Jack intervened, "That's easy. Just separate the ruby from the sceptre and bring it here and destroy it," he smiled happily.

But to his dismay, Jargon said in a deep hissing voice which usually meant that he was speaking something important, "No it's not at all easy. It can be destroyed only by the Holy Sword of Iregor which probably you already possess," he said pointing to me.

I nodded. He continued, "And as you all know that Alex's sword cannot be separated from him, in the same way neither can King Maut's sceptre be separated from him nor can the ruby be separated from him unless he does it on his own," he paused and then asked a question, "Where is the battle being fought?"

Jason answered, "Glore and Lord Theromir decided that it would be fought in the fields of Gorum where our fathers had earlier fought the Great Battle of Gorum."

Jargon said, "So it is all up to you how you bring the ruby here. I cannot help you in that. It's not as easy as it sounds."

"But why cannot the battle be fought here in Iregor?" I asked.

"No, I don't think Lord Theromir will allow that. He will not wish to see the destruction of Iregor. And he's still quite troubled by the invasion of the marketplace of Iregor. I'll be waiting for you here and then I'll give you further instructions."

Roalf arbitrated, "You mean you aren't going to fight alongside us in the war."

"No, I just can't," the answer came swiftly. "I'll be drawn towards my race by loyalty or King Maut will somehow kidnap me and take me with him. And if none of these things happen I will not be able to reach this cave in time because I am much slower than you all."

"Okay," said Roalf, with disappointment in his voice.

"And remember," Jargon said, "that when you carry the ruby here, all your way you'll be tempted to take a long stare at the beauty of the ruby. That would be the last for you on this planet as your souls will be sucked out of you and imprisoned in the ruby and you will be enslaved to King Maut. Your fathers had done that mistake. Don't repeat it. That would be my advice."

"Since you're not taking part in the war could you tell us at least one way in which it would be easy for us to defeat Maut?" I asked.

"Anger is his weakness. Just like you, my dear friend. You have to use it in some way to draw his attention towards you so that you can separate him and the ruby. I'll give you a hint...his crown."

"Thanks but what has it got to do with the crown?"

"Use your imagination," was all he said.

CHAPTER 20

The Battle Fields
of Gorum

*T*he morning emerged calm and peaceful. I gazed out the window resting my hands on the window sill, sipping a large tumbler of warm milk. The wind brushed against my face. My hands got wet due to the falling rain. There was a smell of earth in the air. It mixed with the marvelous aroma of the delicious breakfast.

Down below, the gardeners were taking care of the many royal gardens of the Palace of Iregor. Below the hill, on which the palace was located, lived the Iregorians. It was dissected by various rivers coming down from the mountain. Residences stretched infinitely. I could see no end to Iregor. In between the dwellings, markets were positioned and one such market brought back bad memories.

This was the last day of my stay in Iregor. Fate would decide if I would ever return to Iregor again.

Tomorrow we were to march to war. I was confident but still something worried me.

What if I couldn't fight Maut?

What if I die? And what if I could not destroy the ruby? I had no answers for these questions. I briskly brushed these thoughts out of my mind. Slightly pushing myself away from the window I left my room heading towards the dining area for breakfast.

Jack and Jason were already at the breakfast table along with Roalf and Glore. The King's family had already finished their breakfast. My friends were restlessly waiting for me but it was not long before their impatience vanished.

More food was ordered when I came down as it was already empty. I had to eat alone; my friends were full. The food was delicious. It was an everyday routine of the palace. I gulped the food down my throat. I finished it in no time.

Without saying anything all of us returned to our respective rooms. I knew that my friends were worried too. And in such situations it is always better to leave one alone.

We were advised to rest today. For days, me and my friends have been continually practicing, training each other and sharing each other's strengths and working on weaknesses. Jargon would frequently come and see us practicing. I saw him nodding his head a number of times as if he was judging the intensity of each and every blow.

His eyes looked calm and peaceful but behind those calm eyes Jargon was calculating; calculating our chances of destroying the ruby, winning the war and the chances of our survival. No one, except him, knew the result of his calculations.

I knew that Jargon, the greatest blacksmith of the world, was under great pressure. He knew the consequences that would follow if we fail. He was probably more apprehensive and tensed than us. If I were in his position I would have already gone mad. But he seemed to handle the pressure brilliantly. It was most benevolent of a Giant and also ironical to support mankind for the good of the world.

I no longer considered him a Giant. He was completely opposite to his kin except for his physical features. He was not bloodthirsty as his kin and he was too short to be called a Giant. He did not smell too. I would rather call him a mutant rather than a Giant.

He was not going to accompany us. We already knew that. Elvin Rings also was to stay back with him. If he would come, he would have acted as our strategist because he was the one who had all the information on the weaknesses of the Giants. But he had his own reasons, may be ethical or otherwise.

Jargon hadn't given us much advice. The hint that he had given did not seem to click in my mind. The crown...what relation could the crown possibly have with Maut's temperament? Should I de-crown him somehow? I could not understand the hint.

All preparations for the war had been made. Jargon and Elvin Rings had also worked to prepare some new weapons which were specially designed for certain fierce warriors.

Message was sent to Ferogor and Garyland that we would be marching to war tomorrow. They would meet us right at the battleground where we would put up tents on the fringes. The kings of Ferogor and Garyland had come a couple of times to discuss war strategies with Glore and King Theromir. We, the Lords showed no interest in such meets as the strategy part was left to Glore and Theromir. We trained our minds on destruction of the ruby and the death of Maut and nothing else.

In the absence of Jargon, Glore would be our main strategist. He was a fierce warrior and a magician. No one knew the world better than him. Along with Glore other strategists would be Gondlier and Romeg, his magician friends. There were two more magicians coming from Ferogor and Garyland. Glore had mentioned their names once. The gentleman from Ferogor was Borne and the one from Garyland was Salmon.

There were five magicians and four lords going to war and so there was nothing to fear about. But still one cannot be bombastic.

Silence in Iregor was at its peak. The stress on King Theromir seemed to be at its peak too; natural, for he was the King. But he seemed to have recovered from the shock from the attack. That was good news.

His family would remain in Iregor. Clarus would not be accompanying us as he could not fight. I too wanted Clarus to stay as I didn't want him to get hurt. But he was very adamant. He was bent on coming with us. Jack and Jason told him not to act so stubborn. But he did not stop pleading with us until he was ordered to stay back by his father.

The day dawned early and the whole of Iregor awakened at the same time. The army was ready and we were all set to march towards the battle fields of Gorum.

The army was led by King Theromir. He sat proudly on his horse with his long black hair falling elegantly on his shoulders. His large hand held the hilt of his sword which was kept in its sheath and mightily hung by his belt. His taut muscles, which were exposed due to his chemise being pulled up by the heavy metal armor, gave the swordsmen enough confidence that made them wield the sword. His big, stormy grey eyes were filled with determination and confidence.

We, the lords and Glore and his magician friends, rode just behind the King. The sun was high up in the sky. The air smelled of fresh buns and cakes. The musicians played the victory tune. It made us bold and more eager to reach our objective. Men, women and children stood outside their houses to bid us goodbye. Even the South Iregorians had come to see us off.

We were to take the route from the northern gate as Ganohan was towards the north of Iregor. The northern gate was on the other side of the Egor Mountains.

The streets and roads of Iregor were lined by a mob of Iregorians. They clapped together to encourage us. Ribbons and banners were hung by each house. Iregor was wrapped in the cloth of beauty and confidence which bound our hearts to one another.

As we reached the northern gates Lord Theromir alighted his horse, walked a little distance and then raising his right hand turned towards the Iregorians to address them. "My people, since the day my father died and I became the king, I had always dreamt of this day. But I had never imagined that it would come so soon. I feel proud to stand here and address you. I feel proud to lead the army of Iregor into battle. And I feel proud to say before you that I will return only if I defeat and make perish our sworn enemies."

His voice was loud and clear. The crowd applauded loudly. Trumpets sounded, sticks beat against the rubber of the snares and flutes played the victory tune. The monarch of Iregor raised his hand once again and the tune died. The booming voice of the royal vocal cords was heard again, "I would never have taken the decision of war if not for Roalf, Jason, Jack and Alex. It is a pleasure to have them in Iregor."

The crowd clapped once again. The music commenced once again. Amidst that pleasing noise, the King walked to the gate and tapped on the lock in a random fashion and the gates opened right away. The king mounted his horse. Looking at his subjects he said, "My wife and son will stay back in Iregor. I leave Queen Theresa in charge of Iregor in my absence." Waving his hand to the people of Iregor he moved on ahead, and then out of Iregor. We followed him.

In that atmosphere of fraternity and kinship, the King's subjects were heard to say, "Victory to Iregor. Doom to Ganohan."

As we moved out of Iregor, the war cries were still heard, but they were now murmurs from a distance. The music was fainter and then it perished. Everything changed, once outside Iregor. A strange loneliness crept into my heart as the music died. I felt that I was all by myself. I wished to go back to Iregor and spend a night with the euphonious music. But there was no turning back now.

The landscape changed into undulating plains and grasslands. There were hardly any trees. A river stretched towards our right which was at its lower course. It ran down the Egor Mountains. We could have easily taken a boat or a ship from Iregor. It was a pity we didn't do so! The grass was smooth and soft. A clear, bright sky covered our heads. The odorless warm wind polished our bodies. Summer was at hand...

A day passed. The plains were replaced by plateaus, plateaus by valleys, but nothing having much significance could be seen. The river disappeared. But soon another river took its place. We hadn't reached the battleground yet. The army was huge, so our movement was slow. But I hadn't seen the Giants' army yet. Maybe it was still bigger. Hope of equaling the army of Ganohan was the only option we had.

We took breaks at regular intervals. Almost three-fourths of our army marched on foot. And the horses too needed rest. Gradually a forest came into view. The sight disturbed me. I shuddered slightly. But it looked less dense than the Bulkite forests.

After reaching it we realized that the army would have to be regimented. The path was wide but could not accommodate the whole army. The army was divided into three groups. Michael led the left flank and the right flank was led by Tayl. Each of the flanks moved on a track on either side of the middle path at some distance away from it. The troop in the middle comprised of the Lords, Glore, the other magician fraternity and a part of the army lead by King Theromir.

There was considerable space to walk, no thick canopy and the ground was irradiated by sunlight. In this primeval forest there was no struggle for life. It was completely opposite to the forest where the light ceased. But this one too had its uniqueness. Everything in this forest seemed vulgar. I had an eerie feeling. The place smelled profane.

Tired, I asked, "How far is Gorum?"

"It's near." Glore answered smiling slightly.

"Roalf can you please fly up and verify Glore's estimate?" I asked ignorantly.

Roalf said, "No. I know this forest. It's a small one. We'll be reaching the other side very soon." As we walked deep inside the forest, I sort of had a euphoric feeling. The trees and the bushes around gave me a strong feeling that I'd been here before.

After a while an opening was seen. The feeling became more powerful now. Suddenly sounds…talks of humans could be heard. They looked familiar but I couldn't identify them. Altogether the army stopped abruptly. Jack, alone, dismounted his horse and walked ahead quietly. His feet made no sound and his breathing was composed; exactly like a hunter.

He reached the opening and peeped outside. I could see the change in his expression. His expression betrayed all information his brain was processing at the moment. He joyfully signalled us to come and then sauntered ahead. The army increased its pace in its anxiety. We burst out of the forest to come under the blazing sun.

We were on the crest of a hill. The same river flowed a little distance away from us and went down the hill. I felt euphoric again. My eyes fell on the huge expanse of sandy land below. Then everything fit in my mind like a jigsaw puzzle. This was the same place that I saw in my second dream. We were at the grounds of Gorum.

But what was Jack so happy about? The sounds… they were very prominent now, coming from my right. I turned in the direction and found my fellow companions and the ruler of Iregor greeting the Kings of Ferogor and Garyland. I joined them. We received information that they had come a few hours before and that they had immediately sent lookouts but the Giants were nowhere to be seen. The Kings rejoiced saying that the Giants were scared and could not face us. But Iregor knew better.

King Theromir, before leaving Iregor, had sent a message to Ganohan that Iregor had declared war against the Giants and that it would be fought on the battlegrounds of Gorum three days later. Naturally, they would have been prepared. We did not worry about that.

The army of Ferogor and Garyland had completely occupied the top of the hill. There were countless tents. Consequently, we had to set up tents at the bottom of the hill.

After everyone had settled down I turned my attention to my somnolent body. The journey had exhausted me. It had taken two and half days for us to reach this blasphemous place. I wondered how I would take the ruby away from Maut and destroy it at Iregor.

I disliked this battlefield. It disturbed my thoughts. I could not concentrate. I regretted being at this place. I got tired quickly. It had a weird sort of temptation as if trying to tell you to leave your kin and go beyond Gorum. This was because; maybe it was situated closer to evil, closer to Ganohan?

While I was debating it, my eyelids stretched and closed as I was almost sleepy. I fell into slumber within no time.

It was half past four when I woke up. Work was going on outside. The grounds were so big but still they seemed crowded. Soldiers were feeding the horses in the stables. The King of Iregor was busy too, giving orders and walking everywhere. The Kings of all the three empires going to war frequently met and then, nodding their heads, returned back to their camps.

Jack was busy sharpening his axe. At the practise area I saw Jason practising throwing his spear as if he was aiming at a Giant. Roalf was sitting on a tree at the crest of the hill. He was a small figure at that distance. I somehow recognized him.

I joined him at the branch on which he was sitting. This reminded me of my hateful encounter with the twin Giants – Ronkar and Batchels.

"There's something wrong." The lord of the wind said as I made myself comfortable beside him.

"What's wrong?" I asked.

"I can't feel the Giants." He said worried and thinking.

"So you can even feel the Giants?" I asked astonished.

"No, not like that," he said laughing, "I always get a peculiar feeling when I'm close to Giants."

"Oh. But how can Jack sense the creatures?"

"He cannot sense the Giants. He can only sense if any living thing is at ground at a given distance."

"I have an idea! Could we go and check out the other side of the battlefield?" I asked excited.

"Don't be silly," Rolf slapped my back slightly and then continued, "That would be too dangerous. We don't know what's there on the other side."

"We'll not go too far." I pleaded.

"Okay but only at midnight when everyone's asleep." He said wearily, "Now let me go and get some sleep. I'll wake you up when its time."

I couldn't sleep that night. Maybe that afternoon sleep had not lost its effect on my body. I slept in my tent along with Jack, Jason and Roalf. It was quite congested, but in that state of war, what choice did we have?

Roalf, assuming that I was fast asleep, called on me at the right time. Slowly but steadily, we carefully moved out of the tent. But just as we were exiting, I tripped over Jason's leg and was going to collapse on Jason had not Rolf caught me.

"Careful." He whispered.

"Sorry." I said.

At the stables outside, two soldiers were keeping watch. They had gathered some wood and had made fire which was burning dimly. However, our shadows could be seen easily. Tip-toeing we silently moved past them. The soldiers were drowsy; we were lucky. But not so lucky, two more pairs of soldiers on the hill were also keeping watch. I hoped that they were somnolent too.

We walked on the periphery of the battleground, as suggested by Roalf, because the walls of the plateaus, which surrounded the battleground, would prevent our shadows from coming into view. I could hear the sounds of the river water as it gushed down the hill into the battlefield.

As I walked away from the camps an atypical fear entered my heart. The air had become chilly. The fog was making me shiver. It took us time to reach the other end; the grounds of Gorum were large.

On the other end there was no upliftment of land. A forest began in a short distance. We edged closer to the forest. Roalf was leading now. The surroundings were partially visible in the moonlight. Roalf took a step into the forest and then waved a hand to me. I followed him. An eerie feeling filled my heart.

After walking a few yards Roalf stopped dead. Suddenly I felt as if I was being watched. I felt dreadful. I could sense the creeping of a peculiar feeling in my body. I heard Roalf's whisper, "They're here, watching us."

The chilly wind brushed my face. The peculiar feeling was of déjà vu. My body was tense and ready to wield the sword if the situation demanded. The howling sound of the wind was running through my auditory canal and adding to the eeriness of the situation. A strong smell of garlic in the air awakened our senses. "Watch out." Roalf hollered as something fell ahead of us. A single turn and off we were.

We did not care to check what it was that fell from above. We did not want our curiosity to take the better of us. A good run would have returned us to the battleground in no time. But before we could do so, I felt a net on my head and I was down to the ground. I shrieked in pain. I saw Roalf too struggling with the net.

Ahead of us jumped two giants. I was still lying on the ground. I slowly raised my mud-spattered head. The sight of a vulgarly twisted skin developed a vomiting sensation in my gut. I could feel its graphitic roughness. Their feet looked like wringed out rags. The two feet attached to each leg were perpendicular. The three horns on their head somewhat developed a fear of spikes in me. The body of the giants was opulent with repulsiveness.

I somehow felt as if I had met them before. But I just couldn't get the hold of it. It was their voice that made me sure of who they were.

"What should we do with them?" Batchels asked his brother Ronkar.

"Cook them, that's all. It is better we do so while our kin sleep. No one will notice us."

Roalf engaged them in a conversation. He had worked his way through the net. My sword, that hung by my side, was causing some problem. So I was still fidgeting with the net.

"I've heard a lot about you both; about your bravery." Roalf said.

The giants altogether turned towards Roalf, not just their heads but their whole body. That was due to rigidity in the back of their necks due to the presence of scales. "Of course you would have. We are the favourite twin giants of Maut." The less experienced one said.

"They speak a lot about you two in Iregor; how you two burnt Iregor alive once by your trickery."

Ronkar replied, "Yeah that was quite fun. King Maut rewarded us for that. Those burning flames of Iregor ended our appetite for hatred. The blood and the fresh human flesh caressed our mouths."

That comment was unbearable. I clenched my wrists in anger. Slowly but steadily I managed out of the net while Roalf was keeping them busy. I stood up stout. The giants were still facing Roalf so I was not visible to them. I quietly moved across the path, behind the giants, in the dim glow of the giants.

Once I was behind them, I unobtrusively signalled Roalf. He broke off in the middle of his speech and jumped high in the air and shot arrows at the giants from his partially materialized bow and arrow. The giants stumbled backwards. I sliced my sword through their thick-skinned backs.

The giants were too dumb-struck to react. We were too quick. Within seconds they were wiped off the earth. Finally I had taken my revenge; the one that I had vowed to take in the Bulkite Forests. I had killed Ronkar and Batchels with the help of Roalf.

Done with inspection we returned to the battlefield. As we reached our camps, just escaping a drowsy soldier's view, I felt normal and warm once again. I thought no more of the short escapade. Roalf and I jumped into our tent with a mind that was fully awake now.

CHAPTER 21

The War

*T*he big day had arrived. The army of Iregor, Ferogor and Garyland merged and gathered at the battleground; Iregor in the centre, Garyland to the right and Ferogor to the left. The army was huge enough to fight the Giants; it appeared so to me. The previous night's adventure had been forgotten since I have to be composed and brave today.

Jack and Jason led the army of Garyland and Ferogor respectively as they were the natural descendants and now well known among the masses. Glore and I were left in the middle along with King Theromir. Roalf was with the archers. The Giants were nowhere to be seen. The magicians were fairly distributed all over the combined armies.

The cavalry was at the front. The archers were at the top of the hill from where they would get a better range to wipe out at least one-fourth of the enemies. Massive catapults were set up from which flaring balls of fire would be discharged. Of course, Jason would not be the source of fire there.

With the armour and the helmet on, my body felt heavy. But I had had enough training with it so I was able to carry it on me. The effect of the armour did not slow me down.

King Theromir looked magnificent in his bronze plated armour. The armour was shimmering in the bright sunlight. He sat proudly on his beautiful big brown-white horse. He was a huge man; he needed a huge horse to carry him. I hadn't learned or seen much of his skills. Probably there was more to come from him.

Our weapons were positioned and the army was ready and rearing to go. But the Giants had still not shown themselves. The army was growing restless. I could feel the tension among the masses.

King Theromir shouted out loudly in his booming voice, "Show yourselves you nasty creatures! Do not hide. Shame on you that you can't even fight a war!"

Just then as if in reaction, a huge sand wave came rushing towards us and the ground started shaking. We held our ground steadfastly. The wave died. But I could not see clearly through the cloud of dust. I could sense movement because of the ground vibrations. Slowly when everything became normal I could see a massive army of Giants positioned at a distance ahead us.

King Theromir rode forward and so did two Giants from the opposite side but the Giants marched on ground, they didn't have a suitable horse to carry them;

only a mammoth could carry them. The trio stopped when they were close enough to hear one speak. The King of Iregor stared up at the Giants for a long time. The Giants too stared down at him.

King Theromir asked them loudly, "Where is your King? The ugly beast is hiding, uh? That was an obvious question in my mind too. But I had no time to think about that.

We saw one of the Giant's raise his big mace full of spikes and haul it at the King. That very moment what I saw made me stay stupefied. The mace harmlessly bounced off a shimmering golden barrier which had developed around the king during the course of the Giant's action. I could not believe my eyes. Glore was beside me. He was smiling.

"What's that, Glore?" I asked anxiously.

"That's Theromir. He's taking his true form…You don't really know Theromir enough, my boy," Glore answered with that perpetual smile. I turned and saw Lord Theromir rushing back. He had hardly reached when a battle cry was heard from the other end of the ground.

The Giants charged. It seemed as if a grey forest was moving. The ground was shaking. But we waited because we knew what was going to happen.

The Giants drew closer. King Theromir still waited, and then suddenly he raised his sword high in the sky. A golden beam of light shot out from it which acted as a signal for the archers.

In seconds there was a heavy downpour of arrows on the Giants. Roalf was with the archers, so there was nothing to worry about. Majority of the arrows hit the Giants and killed them instantly as the arrow tips were coated with deadly poison. Some hit the ground and were stepped over by the Giants. A great number of Giants were fallen within no time. But in my mind I knew that the majority of the army, including Maut, had not yet shown up.

There was another battle cry followed by a torrent of burning stones from the other side. I ducked as one was almost going to hit me. "Shields up!" shouted Lord Theromir. We followed the command. Two more shouts from the Kings of Ferogor and Garyland, and the armies followed that command. I bet, if seen from above the combined army would look like a massive shield.

"Catapults!" King Theromir shouted once again. The Giants were counter attacked. The archers stopped firing and flaring balls of fire descended upon the enemies. I lowered my shield and straightened myself.

I was waiting for the King's order to charge. My hands were growing restless. I wanted to use my sword which was beginning to grow warmer in my hand signifying the presence of evil.

I felt the presence of Roalf beside me. He had done splendid work with his bow. A great start for us. His huge gold plated weapon was glowing under the bright sun. On his back hung the quiver containing infinite arrows. Roalf was really a marvel.

Roalf was just going to say something when our leader shouted, "CHARGE!" There was silence for a second and then we charged and roared like lions. Roalf jumped and aimed arrows at the giants. My horse neighed and lunged forward.

I pierced a Giant as it was going to attack me. My heart was filled with pride at the sight of seeing the Giant collapse. This was the first kill of my life. I knew at the moment that there were many more killings to happen by my sword. I had the great burden of destroying the ruby on my shoulders. I had to maintain peace in the world. I was the Lord of water. I had my friends with me but still knew that I had the greatest responsibility.

With these thoughts I fought bravely and tirelessly. I used my powers to cause geysers to toss the giants several metres high in the sky. I was far away from the river but still I could make it obey me. At times I glanced at Jack and Jason. Jack was hurling stones and boulders at the Giants. He used his axe for smashing and chopping the Giants' legs. Jason was burning every Giant that came under his target zone. It was easy to burn the Giants for Jason as their skin was already on fire due to perspiration of phosphorus laden sweat. He was competing with Roalf in slaughtering the Giants. Roalf was flying just above me firing arrows at his targets. He didn't need a horse.

It was going to be dusk as the sun was about to set. The horn sounded portending that the first day of war had ended. Luckily, I had not been injured in any way during this first day. My palms and shoulders had blood stains from fallen giants. The armour saved my upper body but there were gashes on my legs. Giants' blood covered my sword. But its radiance could still be seen.

Though everyone was still raring to go there was nothing one could do except to take rest and treat lesions and wait for the morning sun. My wounds needed a few stitches. It was only the first day and I was filled with pride over the performance of the entire army. This is what I realized war is – bloodshed and nothing else. It is a state of endless suffering and pain. We had already lost many of our soldiers though no one was thinking about it.

Jack and Jason were in the same condition. But it was normal to Roalf as war was not new to him.

A week passed with devastation and more vigorous fighting. The battle had been haphazard. It was ineffable. We were giving an equal challenge to the Giants. Maut had still not shown up. Innumerable had died but the war still continued. We were beleaguered. But amidst all the fracas of the war there was a big problem which I had realized one night. I immediately called a meeting of the Lords along with Glore and Lord Theromir.

"So what's wrong?" It was always Jack who asked this question, but this time it was Jason. I had actually awoken them during their sleep, I could understand the irritation.

"We have a huge problem," I said.

"Come on Alex. This war is the biggest problem that we have. Soldiers are dying; our army is slowly being outnumbered even after considering the forces of

Ferogor and Garyland. We are out of supplies and how much bigger a problem do you want?" King Theromir said with a worried and raised voice. He was under great pressure, of handling the armies.

Yes, he was right. We were out of our supplies. We were struggling to keep on going in this war. The soldiers were suffering from malnourishment and the army was reduced to more than half the original number.

I replied, "How would Jargon know when we would reach the cave with the ruby. He and Elvin Rings are the only ones who know how to cross that barrier that bars the entry to the cavern. He has to keep an open entry for us. How will he know when to keep our entry clear?"

"Good question, Alex. I hadn't even thought of that." Jack suddenly jumped into the conversation.

Roalf said, "Whatever we got to do, we have to do it tomorrow. Everything has to end tomorrow. Our loss is guaranteed if we go on fighting like this."

"I got it." Glore who was quiet for so long, spoke up now. "We can use a portal."

"But how?" Jason asked.

"Leave that to me."

"If that is the case, then can you transfer us directly to Egor Mountains?" I asked.

"No, I can't do that with the ruby in your hand as it is immune to my magic." The magician replied wearily. "But you have to set off for Egor Mountains as soon as possible; that is assuming, Maut shows up and we are able to lay our hands on the ruby. It will take you a day to reach Iregor and make sure to be well ahead of Maut, so that you can rest in between. Let's hope Maut shows up as early as tomorrow. Okay now, goodnight. I am very sleepy." The meeting ended.

The eighth day of the war began in the same way as it had on the first day. There was no progress in the war. It was kind of balanced. Both the sides were losing their men. No one could estimate whether we were going to lose or win.

The trees on the surrounding plateaus were burning. Thousands of bodies lay on the ground by noon. A layer of ash covered the river. My sword was stained with Giant blood. Blood flowed down my cheek. A sword had slashed me over there, lacerating my cheek. For my safety I had worn a helmet but that had been knocked off by another Giant. My cheek was flaring with pain but I had to go on. There was one strange thing – Maut hadn't shown up yet.

And then suddenly, as we were warring the Giants retreated. I was clever enough to understand, so was King Theromir that they were regrouping. He gave the order to retreat and regroup. I remembered my second dream. According to the reverie, this was the stage when Maut shows himself. So I quickly raced down the army to find Jack and Jason and brought them to where Roalf and the king were waiting.

As expected the Giants' army slowly parted into two, revealing the most hideous creature I had ever seen. It was even uglier and pathetic than what I had seen in my first dream. The ground juddered under my feet as it walked on ahead to the centre of the battlefield.

It was about fifteen feet tall. The Giant king had round eyes that looked shut with white membrane, huge elephant ears protruded forward. Emerald coloured spikes jutted out from his body. Three horns jutted out of his head which too had those shining spikes. I heard Jack comment, "What an ugly beast! Is this real?"

That fifteen feet tall monster had a colossal outpouring stomach. It held a sceptre in its hand. A large unblemished ruby was fixed into the sceptre's head. It wore a magnificent crown which too was penetrated by emerald coloured spikes. It surely had a lust for precious stones. The crown... the hint that Jargon had given. I still couldn't know how that crown would help me and how I would remove it from its place. Jason prayed, "Tell me that monster is not Maut."

"Sorry Jason, it is Maut." Roalf said, "Get ready Alex, you have work to do."

"I am." I said without turning my head.

The Giant raised its sceptre slowly. "Alex," I heard Lord Theromir's tensed voice, "Do something quickly. It's going to use that cursed ruby. Only your sword has the ability to oppose it. You've got to protect our army. Quick!"

I didn't understand a thing that the King had said. I had to protect the army. But how? I saw the Giant flip its sceptre and bring it down to the ground. In that fraction of a second, I remembered the flash in my second dream, the moment when the giant had banged its sceptre on the ground and when all sound and light ceased. I knew what to do.

The Giant banged its sceptre on the ground. I did the same. I jumped high and guided my sword deep into the ground, trying to create a shield. It worked. A watery shield extended on both sides of my sword. It stretched endlessly from my sword in many layers in a fraction of a second.

Sound and light ceased. A powerful wave knocked me off my feet but I still held my sword tightly. The wave couldn't cross the barrier. Light returned the next second. I heard a big gasp, which could have come only from Maut.

My watery shield had reflected the shock wave back toward its source. The Giant's unholy army was reduced to an army of just four Giants. The ugly Giant King Maut had caused self-destruction. I couldn't control my laughter. Jack and Jason joined me. I could see its face. It was crestfallen and dumbfounded.

I stopped laughing when Roalf glared at us. We still had worked to do. Maut, alone with the ruby, could destroy us. The army waited behind while we, the Lords charged.

I tried to slash the Giant with my sword. It was blocked. Jack cut its thigh flesh which was the only uncovered part of its body. Jason shot fire from his spear at the Giant's wounded thigh. It shrieked in pain. Roalf was in the air releasing deadly arrows from his bow. Maut was shouting and crying like a mad dog. We fought relentlessly. But I knew that we wouldn't be able to continue fighting like this for a long time.

Therefore I spoke to my friends ahead, "Jack, Jason and Roalf." I didn't care if they understood or not, I couldn't risk getting distracted at that moment. "Move on ahead. I'll be right behind you all. Don't worry about a thing." They understood me and ran back towards our army to go back to Iregor the same way we had come here.

But Maut who was busy fighting me, noticed that moment and created a barrier in front of them. They had no choice but to take the opposite route, climb the plateaus and then turn around to take the longer way. They ran into the forests on the other side.

I noticed the Giant's palm open. I sliced it into two. It yelled in pain. Angry, it knocked the sword from my hand. It went flying into the forests. I tried to pull it towards me but it wouldn't come. Maybe the ruby's evil power was preventing it from coming to me. I looked for my friends. But they had long disappeared into the forests. Now I was without my sword and alone. I had to use my powers. This was the time.

I ran in the direction of the river. Maut ran behind me. I jumped into the river. It was shallow and very narrow. I could breathe inside it. Water was all I needed. I blasted the Giant's face with a rapid jet of water. I fought using water, the Giant with his sceptre. This couldn't continue for long. I had to do something. I was already feeling exhausted. The crown… how could it help me? Anger was Maut's weakness. What relation could a crown have with anger? I thought. What would happen if I remove the crown from the Giant's head? Of course it would get angry, but will it be enough to make it drop the sceptre? May be it will. I realized that any King, beast or man, would lose his temper when his crown is taken away.

I directed a jet burst of water at his crown. I caught it as it was falling down. Man, it was really heavy. The Giant roared loudly. I ran towards the forests. While running I threw the crown into the river. Maut roared even more loudly at the sight. I turned and sped. It was dusk and there was no one to sound the hood to end the war for the day. I was inside the gloomy forests.

The Moon showed up in the sky. The swiftly moving breeze brushed my hair. Oak and Elm trees stretched on either side. The sand under my feet rose in the air due to the breeze which set up a convection current. The dry leaves fallen on the ground however were not swept by the current; these just made a ruffling noise, for a reason. They crumpled under my feet as I ran deep into the forest, tired and panting and armed with nothing except my clothes and armor. Well why wouldn't I run? Maut was chasing me.

Suddenly I realized everything - My first dream was coming true.

I had nick-named it Philips. Ha! How I remembered Mrs. Philips. If you have forgotten her then this is for you: She was my grumpy ex-Science and Math teacher.

I thought Mrs. Philips to be a person who knew nothing about the world but herself. She was similar to Maut. But the only difference was that she lacked a huge Giant like body.

I saw a sword dug deep into the ground nearby a tree but something was written on it. After a moment I realized that it was my weapon – The Holy Sword of Iregor. I gained confidence. I ran faster. If I could just feel the sword back in my hand, I could gain all my energy back.

I also could see what the inscription was; Oh! God... the two words were written in a scrawl– 'by Roalf' were in scripted. I didn't have time to think over it as Maut was getting closer. I was too astonished that I couldn't even get myself moving fast enough. But I knew I had to continue or die in a painful way. For sure I didn't want to take my last breath in the hands of an obese monster.

I moved towards the sword to defend myself from Maut. But before I could reach it I tripped over a rock and fell to the ground with a thud. I shrieked in pain; I was just inches away from my sword. If I could just get hold of it, I would gain all my energy back and be an equal rival for my opponent. I desperately tried to reach its hilt but I couldn't. Maut was advancing towards me. He came nearer and nearer. I tried once again but in vain. I thought hard. I had to do something...Maut was nearing. There had to be something that could help me. I'm sure there was one. I just couldn't remember it.

I went back, in my mind, to the start of this adventure. I remembered how I and my friends had gone underground in the Sumter Fort, how we had found the treasure there. I reminisced how I had met Glore, how he had given me the golden sphere, how he had…Wait a minute. The golden sphere! Glore had given that to me telling that it would help me somehow. Maybe now was that moment when the sphere could help me. That was my only hope. I had to trust Glore. Of course I trusted him, but at that moment one wrong decision would have cost me my life and the world, its peace. To die at the hands of a corpulent monster, was the worst way to succumb.

I imagined it in my hand. It appeared instantly. No difficulty. I handled it heartily. My hands were shaking. I didn't know what to do with it. I knew I would die if I didn't do anything. That was what I saw in my dream. My sword was there near me. Then something inside my soul, urged me to fight; it told me not to give up. It told me that I had to change the situation because I am the Lord of water, the son of Dane.

I felt a shadow on my back. I turned. The moon was blocked from my view when Maut jumped high in the air, with his sceptre right above my heart. In that fraction of a second, I rolled aside with the sphere in my hand. But the sceptre cut through my pants and flesh. Blood spurted out of the torn skin. It flared with pain.

I really was missing Glore. He always had a panacea for every dilemma.

I was still fidgeting with the sphere when it dropped down from my hands. Nothing happened for a moment. Then I heard a sound. I looked at it. The sphere was slowly dismantling itself. I looked at it with awe.

Maut too was watching it with awe. But then he wasted no time in attacking me again. He wielded his scepter once again. This time I ducked just in time and escaped it blow.

The next moment I was knocked down by a force behind me. I turned in anger. It was really making me lose my temper. But it struck me easily this time. Maut was following the similar pattern that Glore had during my training. I knew that this time Maut would hit me on my head. But what could I do. I had no weapon with me. My sword was close by, but I couldn't reach it and it was stuck in ground. There was little chance that it would come to me in the presence of that unholy ruby.

Nevertheless I had to try. I concentrated, trying to draw the holy sword of Iregor towards me, stretching out my hand. I felt the blow. It came early this time. I maintained my balance. I held my ground. I was really losing my nerve. I concentrated even harder. The same urge came to me once again and with that my sword. I turned around and slashed my sword through the air in a swift action. My action met resistance; that was Maut's body. He materialized in front of me and looked surprised as he did not expect to be out maneuvered. But still he was in mood for fun and was holding his stomach and grinning. May be he thought that I was just another young royal kid and did not know the power of the holy sword. My slash hadn't killed him but it had wounded him giving me sufficient time to get away.

At the same time I noticed the golden sphere had dismantled entirely. From it arose a blue orb. The orb expanded into a screen. And on it jumped Glore's face. That dumbfounded me.

"Hey" He said. "Are you okay?"

An excellent idea came to my mind. I spoke quickly, "Yeah, I'm fine. Thank you for the golden sphere. I do not have much time. Maut's behind me, injured a little. Quickly create a portal here leading me to JJR. Will you?"

"That meant Jack, Jason and Roalf, I guess, said Glore. Okay, so here it is." A hollow black portal came into existence beside me. Glore continued, "It will last only for a few seconds. We have sent some men after the Giant."

"That will be of no use. Thank you and see you soon." The screen vanished and the dismantled sphere lay motionless on the ground. I remembered the writings on my sword. I held it up in the moonlight. It was very difficult to read. I strained my eyes. On it was written in blood and in a scrawl, "We are following the course of the river. Make haste."

I prayed that my friends were alright. Blood was a symbol of injury. The portal would exist only for a few seconds, I reminded myself. Everything was done. Maut was injured and I could breathe easy. But there was one thing remaining to do, the most important of all.

I turned around. I had to take the ruby. But how? Jargon had said that Maut cannot be separated by his ruby unless he does it himself. I thought hard, scratching my head. Maut was trying to maintain his balance. He held out his right hand and showed me his fist. A mistake. The sceptre dropped down. I simply picked it up and laughed. He had himself separated the sceptre and the ruby from his body. No time for me to cut it. The portal was diminishing.

The giant yelled, "I'll destroy you! You cannot have the ruby. You do not have the powers."

"Who said that I was going to keep the ruby?" I shouted at him, "I'm going to destroy it. I am not a greedy monster like you Maut. I'm the Lord of water, the son of Dane. My name is Alex."

I turned and walked on to the portal. But I wanted to show off a little. I kept my sword in my sheath. I was in full form and energy. I felt the water under my feet. I raised both of my hands. The water erupted from the ground like a tsunami and I entered the portal with the ruby.

CHAPTER 22

The Final Stage

On the other side, the world was greener; quite different from the battlefield. The black portal camouflaged perfectly with the dark circean night. The ruby in the sceptre was glowing in the dark of night. Its eerie glow blinded me. Every time I looked at it, I felt my soul stirred. Holding it was the last thing you would like to do in this world. I removed my armour and used it to cover the ruby. I was protected against the ruby by the presence of the Holy Sword of Iregor dangling on the side of my waist.

I could see a bonfire at a little distance from me. Around it were Roalf, Jason and Jack sitting. Fire danced on their faces; death had danced beside me just a little while ago. JJR rushed to me as soon as they saw me. "Oh! Alex. I'm so happy to see you. I was almost about to think that you were…" Jason said with happiness.

"Thanks. That beast was quite angry at me. But I survived." I said with a fake smile. I was tired.

"We almost thought of returning back to help you. But Roalf said that you would come. We have been waiting here for a long time. We had almost sought solace in this campfire. All our hopes had wandered off like birds in the night sky." Jack spoke with a smile on his face.

"Don't worry my dear friend." I said hugging him. "None of us will ever fall until this giant ruby is destroyed." I laughed still hugging the Lord of earth tightly.

I continued, "Thank you Roalf, for leaving my sword at the right spot. But how did you know that right spot?"

"Just a guess!" He exclaimed, "Now that you've come, please sit down, rest and tell us your story."

I told them my story. I didn't miss anything. Jason spoke after I'd finished, "I'd completely forgotten about the golden sphere. Good you remembered it."

"That's not important," said Roalf showing a slight irritation, "Where's the ruby?"

"Here." I showed them the sceptre which I was holding in my right hand. Strange they hadn't seen it yet. They came nearer, for either of the two reasons: To have a better view of the ruby or to try to take it from me. I could see the ill effect working on them. Roalf was showing some resistance, he was experienced.

I shoved it away. "I need to keep it covered to protect your souls." I said and covered it with my armour before they could satisfy their curiosity.

My friends returned to normalcy. "Okay that's all for tonight. Sleep. I'll keep a watch. Tomorrow we start early. It will still take half a day to reach Iregor."

"Yeah, we better start early. I've injured Maut. But he'll recover quickly and will be on his way to find me. I'm sure of that." I lied down beside the river.

In the course of this action, my back was exposed and Roalf could see the wound on my back. "Wait a minute. What happened to your back Alex?" He asked inquiringly.

"Nothing." I replied, "The sceptre hit me there." Even as I said, I knew that it was a serious wound. The pain seemed to grow every minute. The ruby's poison had developed roots deep into my body sucking out every bit of power that was left. It infiltrated my nerves. At times I even felt my back turning numb.

"You look so delirious," said the Lord of wind.

He noticed my thigh too and wanted to tend to it immediately. But I gestured to him with my hand to stop, unsheathed my sword and pointed it toward the river. Water was pulled over the sword in a slithery motion and covered my body like a blanket. The wounds somehow vanished into the water blanket and I felt rejuvenated. JJR watched me in merriment.

We chatted away the night and slept in the wee hours.

As decided the previous night, we started as soon as it dawned. Maut was still out of sight. But Jack said that he could feel slight tremors that signified his coming. I swam through the river. Jack ran on the ground, Roalf was flying and Jason was flying too, using his power – the fire blasting out of his palms and feet.

The red glow of the ruby was beginning to show even through the armour. It was an indication that Maut was within the radius of influence of the ruby. It only meant that we have to move faster and away from Maut.

We reached Iregor mid-afternoon. I was not wet under water. Neither did my body ache nor my muscles twitch even after such a long distance swim. Water worked like adrenalin on me. The massive black northern gates were already open. Glore had worked his magic.

We informed the guards to close the gates. Four horses were waiting for us at the base of the mountain. It took us right to the cave. Jargon awaited us at the cave entrance. I could see the anxiety on his pale giant face which had changed into a cheerful smiley on seeing us. I alighted the horse. His eyes immediately fell on the armour draped sceptre. The smiley changed into an expressionless serious face.

"Well done." He said, "Quick come in we have work to do."

On our way inside, Jargon talked, rather quickly, "You took so much time to reach Iregor. What had happened?"

I answered, "I spent a little time with Maut."

"Hope he didn't hurt you."

"He rather did." Jack answered for me.

"Yeah, on his back and thigh." Jason spoke without pity in his voice.

Roalf asked, "I bet it's dangerous. Isn't it Jargon? The ruby has pierced his body. The wound has to be healed quickly. What do you think?"

"It is dangerous indeed. But no need to worry. The effect of the ruby will cease to exist once it is destroyed." Everyone laughed at hearing this. Jargon looked puzzled.

Roalf explained to him about how I was cured by water the previous night. Jargon sighed in relief. But he warned me that the cure was only temporary. Indeed, he was right. I still felt some strange, unanticipated uneasiness in stretching my body.

We came to the brick wall. Jargon drew the pattern on the wall and it slid sideways. Inside we met the blacksmith Elvin Rings. He was even more solemn than he usually was.

To my surprise the podium was on fire. Our shadows danced on the walls of the cavern. I heard the wall moving back to its original place. Jargon spoke, "I hope Maut is chasing you all."

"Yes he is chasing us. But why do you want him to chase us?" Jack questioned inquisitively.

"Because if he does not come here, then you cannot succeed in your mission." Jargon replied.

We gathered around the blazing podium. Jargon's reply had kept me wondering. "There's little time for us to talk. Maut will be coming soon, right to this cavern. Now hear me carefully." The way he spoke was really staid. His faint eyebrows were constricted. A kind of a groove had formed at the place where his nose should have been and the pale face had grown even paler.

He continued, "This stone podium was the place where the ruby was forged. It was on fire at that time and so it is now. It can only be destroyed when it is red hot. But there is one important point."

"It can only be destroyed when Maut is killed…at the same time." Elvin Rings spoke, his voice hoarse as always.

"Yes, Elvin is right. Maut can only die when the ruby is destroyed…at the same instant. After working to forge it for years and studying it secretly, I've understood its nature. Give me the sceptre, will you?"

I raised my hand to give the unholy weapon to the blacksmith. But before I could give it to him Jargon had grabbed it away from me. He was in no mood for etiquette.

"Learn to understand the importance of time, Alex. It's crucial at this critical and final stage." Jargon said with utmost gravity.

He removed the armour and placed the sceptre on the burning podium. The ruby was in the centre. A part of the sceptre extended out of the limits of the podium. I unsheathed my sword to protect everyone from the evil power of the ruby.

The flares on the podium were rising high. It was burning with a lilac flame. Maybe the stone contained potassium. I recalled my chemistry classes at the Flareds

Academy. It had been a long time since I had thought about the Flareds. I didn't need to.

Suddenly Jack jumped up saying, "I can feel him. Maut's nearing. He's almost reached the mountain. How did he pass through the gates?"

"He must have broken them." Jason said as if it was obvious. I hadn't paid much attention to my friends because we were naturally and eagerly expecting Maut.

Jargon spoke even more quickly now, gasping for breath now and then. What's wrong with him? I thought. Maybe he was worried, or was he scared of facing Maut?

"Now listen. Everyone excluding Alex stand by that wall. All four of you have to strike at the same time - that's the key to put an end to him and the ruby. Jack you'll give the count. Your final count will be the count when he breaks this wall. I have no more to say. This final stage depends on you four. It's all about timing-"

Suddenly his eyes fell on the burning podium. The fire was slowly losing its energy. The lilac fire, its flames dancing like a snake, was slowly going down.

Jargon cursed under his breath and hurried towards the corner of the cavern. Elvin Rings understood the reason for the hurry and picked up some small logs of wood beside him.

He ran towards the podium and bent down. I could see his hand movements; it seemed as if he was pushing those logs. He got up with none of them in his hand. Where did all the wood go? I wondered.

The fire burnt more brightly. It seemed to revive its energy. I took my position, by the podium. Then I could see the place where the logs had been pushed. It was a round hole. It was such a shame that I hadn't noticed that clearly visible hole before. Something told me that this cavern had many secrets inside it. I had to discover it one by one.

"You're…a…cow…ard. You…will ne…ver succ…eed." My eyes drifted towards the ruby on the depression. The sound had come from there, I was sure. The voice… it had been dragged.

I heard it again, "Ye…s it's m…e. I'm spea…king t…o you." I fixed my eyes on the ruby. That was the source. I don't know why but I felt a bizarre shroud of fear around me. I opened my mouth to speak but in vain. I couldn't even move my lips. I tried to raise my sword. Neither could I move it nor could I feel it. My concentration was beginning to break.

I knew that I was the only one who could hear the ruby. Therefore I tried to speak through my mind. "Shut up." I said.

"But tell me, what would you get from destroying me?" The voice had no more dragging effect. I could hear it. Its accent was unfamiliar to me.

"There will be peace in this world when dirty desert mites like you will be knocked off from earth."

"But what would you gain from bringing peace to the world." The voice spoke with a bit of provocation. I stayed silent. This was a question worth receiving no attention at all.

I heard a laugh. "Nothing is the answer. Let's join hands. We'll rule the world together and -"

Its speech was broken by a loud and confident Jack's voice. "Alex, Maut's nearing. Get ready." I thanked Jack for bringing me back to this world. The hypnotic effect of the ruby had broken. I felt the sword in my hand once again. My hand was steady with a new kind of potence. My sword was glowing even in the presence of the lilac flames. The watery blue aura reassured me that I was going to succeed.

I took a precocious sleighing stance. I felt the tremors. They were intense. Jack counted, "One, two and three!" With all my power I slashed the sword through the fire until I met a resistance. I had done it in the blink of an eye and in another blink I was there, resting against the wall, hurled by an unknown force. My sword was in my hand.

My eyes were open but they were blind due to immense dust and smoke. There was an unknown strong smell in the cavern. I lay there, by the wall, sodden in sweat and weariness. I knew in my heart that I had succeeded in destroying the ruby.

When the smoke cleared I got up, taking the wall's support. I stumbled but maintained my balance. My body ached with pain. I hadn't realized it when I was sitting. It was difficult for me to breathe. I gasped for breath every now and then.

I joined hands with Jack, Jason and Roalf. Jargon was standing by the podium. It was still burning. Jargon was beaming in his dirty and dusty outfit. He held my armour in his hand. It was glowing red from inside.

"This is the liquid ruby." He said.

"How did it change its state?" I asked.

"The temperature achieved by your blow and the fire was high enough for it to melt." Elvin Rings replied.

"How do we destroy it?" I asked.

"It cannot be destroyed." Jargon said drily. Suddenly in that victory mood, I sensed astonishment and agony among the Lords. We had worked so hard building our bodies only to destroy the ruby. Now after trying our luck we get to know that the ruby cannot be destroyed entirely. This was ironical.

Then Elvin Rings said, "There is no need to destroy it. It has already got converted into the normal precious stone it was before being forged." Okay, a little peace. The ruby was no longer the evil, lethal weapon.

"You have done a great job, all of you. The Giant King Maut is dead." Jargon said pointing behind us. We turned and looked behind. The Giant lay there with its mouth open. As we stared at it, it slowly crumpled into dust. I heard a noise, the sceptre. It too had disintegrated into dust on falling down.

Our great adventure had come to its climax. We had travelled to Ganohan. The portal had appeared at the right time in the cavern. It had been a pleasant surprise to Jargon. He was made the king. All the Ganohonian crowning ceremonies had been performed. It was boring but I was patient. I had seen the masses. They seemed innocent. Jargon was right after all, all of us are the same internally but different externally. Maybe even Ganohonians wanted their king to die. But that was most improbable because Jargon had mentioned that Maut was as good to his people as Lord Theromir was.

"Hey, getting bored?" Jason asked.

"Yeah, but Jargon has done so much for us, I can at least be patient." I replied.

"Don't worry, Alex. We'll reach Iregor very soon." Jack assured me.

Roalf said in his humorous way, "And then you can eat as many grapes as you want." We all laughed together. Grapes were my favourite fruit.

Many parties and festivals were held in Iregor, Ferogor and Garyland. We were grateful to Ferogor and Garyland for their support in the war. Whole of Iregor was dancing in victory. Jargon stayed in Iregor for a few days. A meeting was held for deciding the fate of the liquid ruby. Every time it took up a solid form, Jargon had been forced to reconvert it into liquid. The meeting came to the conclusion that the ruby would form a part of the royal treasury of Iregor. It was so done.

I rested my hands on the window sill and looked out of the window. The plants in the royal gardens were booming with all their glory, gleaming with dew drops. Beyond that, in the main town, the markets were smiling with affection in purple and blue. The rooftops were burning red in triumph under the bright sun.

There was concord finally. Everything had at last come to an end. We had attained victory but still it was pyrrhic. Many of our soldiers had died. They had given up their life fighting for peace. Nothing could heal that deep wound. They would be remembered all over in the western world.

I had seen the aftermath and anguish of war. The only outcome was bloodshed. There was no winner and no looser. I had seen the pain and affliction caused due to separation from loved ones – a bond which when broken, could never be made again.

We had destroyed the ruby and also killed the Giant King Maut. I had killed Ronkar and Batchels with the help of Roalf, and also sort of conquered Ganohan. But then it's me – Alex. So nothing was impossible for the Lord of Water.

Wait, am I boasting too much here? Yeah, I am. Let me tell you, that I wouldn't have done any of the above without the presence of my friends. If not for my friends, I would have spent time in Fymland feeding on grapes most of the time!

We, the JARJ (Jason, Alex, Roalf and Jack) practiced every day getting more powerful. The world could now rest in peace. We had finally discovered the meaning of our life. We had a big purpose in this world. I dreamed to travel this sphere. Glore said that there was a whole new world beyond the sea. I wanted to ride the seas and discover places. Maybe I will do so in the near future.

The combined army was not needed now but it was forever ready to fight any evil that dared to rise. That was enough for the present.

I quietly walked out of the room with the chirping of birds providing a perfect background music to the stillness of nature.

Printed in the United States
By Bookmasters